Jacob Two-Two's
First Spy Case

ALSO BY MORDECAI RICHLER

Jacob Two-Two's First Spy Case

by Mordecai Richler

illustrated by Norman Eyolfson

Scholastic Canada Ltd.

For Daniel, Noah, Emma, Marfa, and Jacob.

Scholastic Canada Ltd.
604 King Street West, Toronto, Ontario M5V 1E1, Canada

Scholastic Inc.
557 Broadway, New York, NY 10012, USA

Scholastic Australia Pty Limited
PO Box 579, Gosford, NSW 2250, Australia

Scholastic New Zealand Limited
Private Bag 94407, Greenmount, Auckland, New Zealand

Scholastic Children's Books
Euston House, 24 Eversholt Street, London NW1 1DB, UK

Jacob Two-Two's First Spy Case Text © 1995 Mordecai Richler,
Illustrations © 1995 Norman Eyolfson, published by arrangement
with Tundra, Inc., Toronto, Canada. All rights reserved.

ISBN 0-439-93812-0

6 5 4 3 2 1   Printed in Canada   06 07 08 09 10

Spy. One who spies upon or watches a person secretly; a secret agent whose business it is to keep a person, place, etc., under close observation.

Clairvoyant. A person who can mentally see objects at a distance or concealed from sight.

Gamble. To play games of chance for money.

FEATURING

IN ORDER OF APPEARANCE

CHILD POWER'S DYNAMIC DUO

THE INTREPID SHAPIRO AND THE FEARLESS O'TOOLE;

MR. DINGLEBAT, THE FAMOUS MASTER SPY;

MISS SOUR PICKLE;

MR. I.M. GREEDYGUTS;

PERFECTLY LOATHSOME LEO LOUSE AND HIS MISERLY MUM.

AND

INTRODUCING

"THE CLAIRVOYANT'S GAMBLE"

WHICH

ONCE MASTERED

WILL ENABLE YOU TO AMAZE YOUR FRIENDS!!!

Chapter 1

Once there was a boy called Jacob Two-Two. He was two times two times two years old. He had two older sisters, Emma and Marfa, and two older brothers, Daniel and Noah. He was nicknamed Two-Two because, as he himself admitted, "I am the littlest in the family. Nobody hears what I say the first time. They only pay attention if I say things two times."

Jacob Two-Two used to live in a rambling old house on Kingston Hill, in Surrey, England, but one day his family sailed across the ocean on a big ship and moved into another rambling old house, this one in Montreal, Canada, where Jacob Two-Two's parents had been born in what Marfa called olden times.

"You'll never believe this, Jacob," said Emma, "but when Mummy and Daddy were kids there was no television, or jet airplanes, or computer games, or even take-out pizza."

"Nobody had heard of the Rolling Stones yet," said Daniel.

"And in those bygone days," said Noah, "only farmers wore jeans. How about that, Jacob?"

"Well, I don't know," said Jacob Two-Two, because he could never be sure that Noah was telling the truth. Once, when Jacob was a mere two plus two years old, Noah had led him to the globe of the world in his father's library, pointed out Australia on the bottom, and told him that the upsidedown people in that country had to wear special magnetic shoes lest they fall into outer space, landing — bumpety-bump — on the planet Venus, where little kids who were still too young to be allowed to watch a horror movie on TV, ride a two-wheel bike, or stay home alone, had to serve breakfast in bed to their older brothers and sisters every morning.

"Or the planet Pluto," said Marfa, "where all that the youngest in the family ever got to eat for breakfast, lunch, and dinner was broccoli."

"Yuck," said Jacob Two-Two. "Yuck."

The older he got, it seemed to Jacob Two-Two, the more difficult and complicated his life became. Once he had been appreciated, but not any longer. In the good old days, before he was even two plus two years old, all he had to do to amaze everybody in the family was to use a knife and fork, or tie his own shoelaces, but these achievements were no longer considered such a big deal. Nowadays he was expected to run errands, rake leaves in autumn and shovel a path through the snow in winter, help clear the table after dinner without breaking a plate, and put away his toys at night. He was expected to do all these things, but his two older brothers and two older sisters still considered him to be a nuisance.

Daniel would kick him out of the living room whenever his friends came round to listen to records or just to shoot the breeze.

"Why can't I stay?" Jacob Two-Two would ask twice.

"Because we'd have to watch what we were saying if there was an innocent kid in the room."

Marfa wouldn't allow him into her bedroom if she was going to paint her toenails or try out different hairstyles in the mirror, which seemed to be most of the time.

Noah and Emma wouldn't let him into their CHILD POWER Command Tent in the backyard unless he paid an entry fee. There they would sit, those two bigshots, wearing bath towels draped over their shoulders like capes, plastic swords fastened to their belts, drinking cranberry juice out of a wine bottle left over from their parents' last dinner party, pretending to be the dynamic duo, the fearless O'Toole and the intrepid Shapiro, who struck fear into the hearts of big people who didn't like children.

"May I come in?" Jacob Two-Two asked one afternoon. "May I come in?"

"That depends," said Emma.

"What did you bring us?" asked Noah.

"I've got two slices of Mummy's apple turnover cake."

"Did you bring forks?"

"I forgot."

"Can't you do *anything* right, Jacob?"

No. Or so it seemed to Jacob Two-Two. And nowadays he also had to stick up for his parents, whom he loved, to Daniel, Noah, Emma, and Marfa.

"They're always going kissy-kissy in the kitchen," said Marfa, "*at their age.*"

"So what?" said Jacob Two-Two. "So what?"

"They're so boring," said Daniel.

"Why do you say that?" asked Jacob Two-Two. "Why?"

"I have to apologize for Mummy at school," said Emma, "because she hasn't got a career, but is always at home teaching us things, reading us stories, cooking and stuff."

"What's wrong with that?" asked Jacob Two-Two.

"It's disgustingly old-fashioned," said Marfa, "but you're still too young to understand such things."

"And Daddy doesn't even go to work like real dads," said Noah. "Instead he's always banging away on that prehistoric typewriter of his upstairs."

He worked very hard, said Jacob Two-Two's mother, to provide for them. But one day when Jacob climbed up to his father's office, which was on the top floor of the house, to investigate . . . *he found him snoring on his sofa.*

"I thought you worked very hard in here to provide for us," said Jacob Two-Two.

"Oh, but I do," said his father, rubbing his eyes.

"You were asleep," said Jacob Two-Two. "You were asleep."

"I was only pretending to be asleep," said his father. "Actually, I was thinking, which is a big part of a writer's job."

"What's a writer?" asked Jacob Two-Two twice.

"Well now," said his father, settling in at his desk and lifting Jacob Two-Two onto his lap, "the truth is I'm a master of magic, sort of."

"How come? How come?"

"Count the letters on my typewriter, Jacob."

There were twenty-six.

"Every morning I come up here," said his father, "toss these letters up into the air, and when they come down again I sort them out, and then there's enough money to buy hot dogs, cross-country skis, ice cream, red roses for Mummy, and maybe enough left over for a bottle of decent single-malt whisky for your devoted, ever-loving, incomparable Dad."

The very next day a reporter from Montreal's *Daily Doze* came to interview Jacob Two-Two's father about his latest book. Pretending to be modest, which was awfully difficult for him, Jacob Two-Two's father told the reporter, "My new book is the best I could do, given my limited abilities." But when the reporter, escorted by Jacob Two-Two's father, passed through the living room, he paused and asked Jacob, "What's it like being the son of a scribbler, kiddo?"

"My daddy's no scribbler," said Jacob Two-Two. "He's a master of magic."

"Oh, yeah," snarled the reporter. "How come?"

"There are only twenty-six letters on his typewriter," said Jacob Two-Two. "And every morning he tosses them into the air, and when they land he just sorts them out and then there's enough money to buy himself a bottle of whisky and some things for us."

The headline on the book page of the next morning's *Daily Doze* read:

LOCAL SCRIBBLER CLAIMS TO BE MAGICIAN
Misleads Innocent Child

Alongside, there was a cartoon of Jacob Two-Two's tottering father, wearing a magician's tattered robes, holding a broken wand in one hand and a bottle of whisky in the other.

"Oooh," said Jacob Two-Two's father, rocking his head in his hands. "After all the sacrifices I've made for you, Jake, look what you've gone and done."

"Serves you right for being such a braggart," said Jacob Two-Two's mother.

Daniel, Noah, Emma, and Marfa agreed. But Jacob Two-Two was tearful. Once more he had meant well but had done something wrong. "I'm sorry, Daddy. Really I am."

"Oh well, I guess I'll drive you to school anyway," said his father, taking Jacob Two-Two by the hand.

No sooner did they open the front door than they were greeted by a surprise. A moving van was parked in front of the house next door, which had been vacant for months. Jacob

Two-Two and his father watched, spellbound, as the movers began to unload items which seemed very unusual, to say the least. Three crates of carrier pigeons. A huge telescope. A clothing rack, possibly ten feet long, laden with military uniforms from all nations as well as other costumes. A trunk so heavy it had to be carried by two men: SECRET CODES, EYES ONLY was imprinted on its side. Not one, not two, but three barrels labeled THIS SIDE UP, INVISIBLE INK. An enormous crate marked MILITARY SECRETS AT REDUCED PRICES, another marked DISGUISES, and a third identified only by the warning KEEP TIGHTLY SEALED AT ALL TIMES. Then a wiry old man, his smile jolly, leaped out of the cab of the moving van. He was wearing a pith helmet, a safari suit, and jungle boots.

"Oh dear," said Jacob Two-Two's father, "that must be our new neighbor."

The new neighbor summoned one of the movers, had him lean an extension ladder against the wall of his house, and then scampered to the top and climbed in through a second-floor window. A minute later he came bounding out of the front door, beaming at Jacob Two-Two, and he sang out, "*Bonjour. Shalom. Buenos dias.*"

"Why did you go into your house like that?" asked Jacob Two-Two, already enchanted.

"Lesson number one, *amigo.* Never enter a new, insecure dwelling the way they'd expect you to. By slipping in through a second-floor window you can surprise anybody lying in wait

for you downstairs. I can tell we are going to be friends," he said.

"Oh, yes," said Jacob Two-Two. "Oh, yes!"

"I am a world traveler. A man who has done many astounding things. I have had a bath in Turkey and eaten turkey in a city called Bath. I once gobbled a sandwich in the town of Rainy River and later waded in a rainy river in the Sandwich Islands. You are looking at a chap who once went out with a fair maiden called Florence in the city of Adelaide, and then kept company with another, called Adelaide, in the city of Florence. I have, in my time, gorged myself on Toulouse sausages in the Canary Islands and kept a canary in a city called Toulouse. Long ago, in my days as a struggling young man, I went hungry in the city of Hamburg, but, by Jove, I lived to eat hamburgers in Hungary," he said, and then he handed Jacob Two-Two his card. It read:

X. BARNABY DINGLEBAT
Master Spy
No Job Too Small
Free Estimates On Request.

Chapter 2

Now that he was two times two times two years old, Jacob Two-Two had to attend an expensive private school for boys called Privilege House, where his best friends were called Mickey, Robby, and Chris. And where his only problem was the ill-tempered Miss Sour Pickle, his geography teacher, who insisted on absolute silence in her class. One day, writing something on the blackboard, her back turned to the class, she suddenly whirled around and demanded, *"What's that terrible racket I hear?"*

"We're breathing, Miss Sour Pickle," said Jacob Two-Two.

"Well, I suppose you must. Even in geography class. But not so loud, please. It's bringing on one of my headaches."

Another day she caught Robby wearing the Number 99 sweater of the Los Angeles Kings in her class. "Hockey is not a sport," she said. "It's violence on ice. Wayne Gretzky. Number 99. Remove that sweater at once, Robby."

The boys were delighted to discover that she knew Wayne Gretzky's name.

"Are you a hockey fan, Miss Sour Pickle?" asked Chris.

"Certainly not," she said. "Why, not one of those brutal, overpaid hooligans could tell me the population of Sri Lanka, or what is the average annual rainfall on the Island of Orkney."

Miss Sour Pickle enjoyed nothing more than sneaking up behind Jacob when he was daydreaming and demanding that he rattle off, in short order, the names of the capital cities of, say, Albania, Libya, and Tibet, or that he stay in for an hour after school.

Miss Sour Pickle aside, Jacob Two-Two got on just fine with everybody at Privilege House.

Then something happened.

After his father drove him to school, the very morning that Mr. Dinglebat became their new next-door neighbor, Jacob Two-Two was in for a second, less welcome surprise. A school assembly had been called. Mr. Goodbody, their gentle head-master, announced he was retiring. "The directors of Privilege House, in their wisdom," he said, biting back tears, "have appointed Mr. I.M. Greedyguts as your new headmaster. Mr. Greedyguts is the distinguished author of several books, including *Spare the Rod and Spoil the Child*. During his army years, he was a sergeant-major in the military police and, following that," he added, weeping openly now, "he was a prison warden."

Next, Mr. I.M. Greedyguts waddled onto the stage, huffing and puffing, his triple chins wobbling. He was so fat, it seemed to Jacob that he had been blown up with a bicycle pump. Munching on a foot-long submarine sandwich, he glared at the boys and said, "Wandering round the schoolyard this morning, I noticed several boys with their shirt-tails hanging out. Or missing buttons from their jackets. Or with socks falling down around their ankles. I saw boys with faces unwashed and with shoes unshined. From now on these offenders will report to my office for punishment. I also wish to announce that I have fired the school cook, Mrs. Bountiful, and hired a new caterer to provide the meals for Privilege House."

When school was out that afternoon, Jacob Two-Two had his third surprise of the day. A panel truck was parked outside and the sign printed on both sides of it read:

PERFECTLY ADORABLE LEO LOUSE'S SCHOOL MEALS
GUARANTEED YUMMY BEYOND COMPARE

Oh, no, thought Jacob Two-Two. *Oh, no. Not Perfectly Loathsome Leo Louse*, who came to their house every Friday night to join in his father's weekly poker game.

Chapter 3

Jacob Two-Two's mother disliked Perfectly Loathsome Leo Louse even more than he did. "Must we have that awful man in our house again?" she asked.

"I've known him for what seems like a hundred years," said Jacob Two-Two's father, "and Perfectly Loathsome Leo never gets invited anywhere else."

"No wonder," said Jacob Two-Two's mother.

Perfectly Loathsome Leo Louse's suit was so shiny you could just about see your reflection in it. His shirt collar and cuffs were badly frayed. He used a rope, instead of a belt, to hold up his trousers. One of his socks was brown, and the other black, to match his smelly shoes, one black, the other brown. He had never married, because a wife would be too costly, as would children, always growing out of their clothes, and he didn't bathe very often either, because soap was so expensive.

"He's so mean," one of the poker players once said, "he wouldn't help a man off a hot stove unless there was some gain in it for him."

"He has the first dollar he ever earned," said Jacob Two-Two's father.

Whenever he came to the house, Perfectly Loathsome Leo Louse would pretend to be fond of Jacob Two-Two when the other men were around, but played nasty tricks on him if he caught him alone. That very evening, for instance, as Perfectly Loathsome Leo Louse approached the house for the poker game, he came upon Jacob watering the front lawn. "My God," he said, "do you still live here?"

"Why not? Why not?"

"Your mother told me she was having you exchanged for a girl. Maybe the deal hasn't come through yet."

Later he caught Jacob Two-Two alone in the kitchen and immediately indicated an imaginary spot on his shirt. "Hey, is that a bumblebee I see there?" And when Jacob Two-Two lowered his head to look, Perfectly Loathsome Leo flicked Jacob's nose hard with his bent finger. "Gotcha, didn't I?"

Because he was such a miser, the other poker players, including Jacob's father, tried their best to beat him in the game. But, unlike the other men, who came to have fun and trade stories about the good old days, Perfectly Loathsome Leo was a very careful player, and that night, as usual, he ended up being a big winner. Whooping with joy as he scooped up his money, he then looked longingly at the food that remained on platters on a sideboard, and said, "Oh, I didn't have time to shop today. Do you mind if I take home enough food for my lunch tomorrow?" And then, without waiting for an answer, he wrapped up enough smoked salmon, salami, ham, potato salad, and coleslaw to last him the rest of the week. Next he turned to Jacob Two-Two's father, and asked, "Are you, um, through with this morning's newspaper?"

"Take it," said Jacob Two-Two's father, laughing out loud.

"Anybody driving my way?" asked Perfectly Loathsome Leo Louse.

"Now that you've got all our money," said one of the players, "why don't we call you a taxi?"

"Oh, no!" protested Perfectly Loathsome Leo Louse, alarmed. "I'll walk."

"Don't worry," said the player. "I'll drive you."

Once Perfectly Loathsome Leo Louse had gone, Jacob Two-Two's mother opened up all the dining-room windows to air things out. "I will never understand why you put up with that man," she said to Jacob Two-Two's father.

"Because Leo's an original," said Jacob Two-Two's father. "There's nobody else quite like him."

"Thank God for that," said Jacob Two-Two's mother.

Chapter 4

Late the next afternoon, everybody in the family was gathered in the living room, except for Jacob Two-Two's mother, who was busy, as usual, preparing a delicious dinner for them.

Jacob Two-Two's father was lying on the sofa, also as usual, reading the latest spy novel by John le Carré. Suddenly he set down his book, and called out in a loud voice, "WHO IS MY FAVORITE CHILD?"

Daniel immediately hid behind the curtains.

Noah made for the nearest closet.

Emma dove behind the sofa.

Marfa slid under the coffee table.

And Jacob Two-Two crawled under a chair.

"I am burdened with five kids," their father said, "four of them ungrateful, lazy beyond compare, each one capable of eating through a basket of peaches in an hour, ordering the most expensive dish on the menu if I take them out to dinner, always forgetting to give me my phone messages, and — the worst offense of all —*failing to laugh at my jokes.* However, my four stinkers aside, I am also blessed with one child who is totally lovable. Obliging. Respectful. Eager to help at all times. But who is it? Where is it? Hmmmn. Let me see. Isn't that a pair of feet I see sticking out from under a chair?"

Oh, no, thought Jacob Two-Two, *not me this time.* But it was too late. He was being dragged out of his hiding place.

"Ah, there you are," said his father. "My favorite child."

Jacob Two-Two groaned. "What do I have to do, Daddy?"

"Wash my car, you lucky devil."

Now that it was safe, the other kids emerged from their hiding places, and poor Jacob Two-Two trudged out of the living room. Then he filled a bucket with soapy water, lugged it out to the driveway, and began to wash the car. He had only been at it for five minutes when he noticed somebody approaching the house next door. The person was struggling along on high-heeled shoes, carrying a handbag, wearing a

19

wide-brimmed straw hat with a cluster of cloth flowers pinned to it, and a floral dress.

"Hiya there, Mr. Dinglebat," said a delighted Jacob Two-Two. "Hiya there."

"Darn it," said Mr. Dinglebat, stamping his foot. "I thought this disguise was perfect. How did you recognize me?"

"But I'd recognize you anywhere," said Jacob Two-Two. "I've been looking out for you ever since you moved in last Monday, and I'm really, really glad to see you again."

"Why thank you, dear boy, *merci beaucoup, gracias*, because I've had many a narrow scrape since we first met."

"Gosh," said Jacob Two-Two. "Gosh."

"I was kicked by a horse in Thunder Bay and saw the dawn come up like thunder in Kicking Horse Pass. One day out there in the wilds, I was obliged to dine on porcupine in the Peace River country, but I found peace at last in the Porcupine Hills. And now, *amigo*, I must get some shut-eye."

The amazing Mr. Dinglebat reached into his handbag, pulled out a bottle and popped its cork, which inflated a huge air balloon. Holding on tightly to its drawstring, he floated up to his second-floor window, paused, and called down to Jacob Two-Two. "On second thought, once you've finished washing your father's car, why don't you visit me in my new abode? I will show you some souvenirs of my many triumphs and teach you a thing or two about spycraft."

Jacob Two-Two, going about his work with newfound enthusiasm, was done in a jiffy, and then hurried over to

Mr. Dinglebat's house. There he was shown a number of fantastic things, things he couldn't wait to get home and tell his sisters and brothers about. And just before he left, not wanting to be late for dinner, Mr. Dinglebat slipped him an envelope marked:

TOP SECRET

FOR YOUR EYES ONLY

"I should warn you," he whispered, "that the letter inside is written in mirror code. That means you will only be able to make sense out of it by holding it up to a mirror. I enjoyed your visit."

"Me, too," said Jacob Two-Two. "Me, too."

"Come again, soon."

"Yes, please!"

Chapter 5

His TOP SECRET letter hidden inside his shirt, Jacob Two-Two ran home and made immediately for the first-floor bathroom, where there was a huge mirror. The door was locked.

"Buzz off," said Noah.

Then he dashed upstairs to try the bathroom on the second floor, where there was also a mirror — and privacy!— available. That door was also locked.

"Beat it," said Emma.

Entering the living room, out of breath, frustrated, and still flushed with excitement, Jacob Two-Two told his father about some of the fantastic things he had seen and heard at the home of their new neighbor, the master spy.

"Nonsense," said Jacob Two-Two's father. "Mr. Dinglebat appears to be just a somewhat goofy, but harmless old man, who enjoys wearing disguises. But a master spy? Not on your life, Jacob."

"Then how come he has a letter from Her Majesty, Queen Elizabeth, praising him for bravery in action?"

"Have you seen the letter?"

"What letter?" asked Daniel, barging into the living room, followed by Noah, Emma, and Marfa.

"Never mind," said Jacob Two-Two. "Never mind. Excuse me, I have to go to the toilet."

"Aw, come on," said his father. "Have you seen the letter?"

"Yes! Yes!"

"What did it say?"

"I can't tell. I can't tell."

"Is it a secret?"

"If it is," said Marfa, smiling sweetly, "you can certainly trust me."

"And me," said Noah, who was wearing his fearless O'Toole costume.

Jacob Two-Two bit his lip.

"Is it a secret or not?" asked their father again.

"Not exactly. Not exactly."

"Why can't you tell us what it said, then?" asked Emma, who was attired in her intrepid Shapiro outfit.

"I think I'd better go and wash my hands before dinner," said Jacob Two-Two, leaping out of his chair.

"Come on," said Daniel, shoving him back into his chair.

"I can't tell you because it was written in invisible ink," said Jacob Two-Two twice.

Daniel whistled.

"Wow," said Noah.

"And he has another letter," said Jacob Two-Two, his cheeks burning red, "this one from the president of the United States of America, thanking him for preventing World Wars Three, Four, and Five from breaking out."

"What did the president's letter say, Jacob?" asked his father.

"I can't tell you. I can't tell you. Now if you'll please, please excuse me."

"Oh, sit down," said his father. "You mean to say this one was also written in invisible ink?"

"No," said Jacob Two-Two impatiently.

"What then?" asked Noah.

"*I was talking to Daddy*," said Jacob Two-Two.

"Aw, come on," said Daniel. "We're all family here."

"Okay, okay," said Jacob Two-Two, heaving a great sigh. "I can't tell you what the president's letter said, because it was written in code."

"Imagine that!"

"Yeah. Imagine that," said Jacob Two-Two. "And he has a sword cane, a cigarette lighter that squirts hot pepper, a secret code book, a tape recorder the size of a small bar of soap that fits into a shoe he has with a hollow heel, and a signet ring that holds a container of itching powder."

"But anybody can buy those things, Jacob," said his father, lifting him onto his lap.

Jacob Two-Two wiggled free. "Mr. Dinglebat is a master spy and that's what I'm going to be when I grow up."

"Jacob, do you know what a spy is, exactly?"

"Sort of. Sort of. *And now, if you don't mind, I'm going to wash my hands.*"

"Hold on a minute," said Jacob Two-Two's father, and, taking him by the hand, he led him into the library and dug out his Oxford English Dictionary, and read aloud to him that "spy" meant, "One who spies or watches a person secretly; a secret agent whose business it is to keep a person, place, etc., under close observation . . ."

Then Jacob Two-Two's mother came in and announced, "Dinner, everybody!"

"Oh, I think I'd just better wash my hands before I sit down," said Jacob Two-Two.

"Now there's a good boy," said Jacob Two-Two's mother, surprised that he didn't have to be asked to do it.

"Yeah," said Jacob Two-Two, and he raced for the first-floor bathroom, locked the door, pulled out his TOP SECRET letter and held it up to the mirror at last.

Chapter 6

MIRROR CODE MESSAGE

The information contained in this message is confidential and is intended only for the use of the individual or entity to whom it is addressed.

TO: JACOB TWO-TWO

FROM: X. BARNABY DINGLEBAT, MASTER SPY

Rules governing visits to X. Barnaby
Dinglebat's "safe" house, which is a dwelling
whose exact location is unknown to enemy
agents, bill collectors, dentists, teachers
who are sour as crab apples, party-poopers,
garden skunks, and all other undesirables.

Trainee spies are not allowed to turn up at
the master spy's house just like that. Watch
for secret signs that only a very observant
lad trained in spycraft can detect.

1. A yellow balloon tied to the trunk of the
maple tree in my front lawn means I am away
on a secret and undoubtedly dangerous mission.

2. If a bunch of bananas is hanging from
the knocker on my front door it means you are
not welcome. I am either

a) hard at work on the story of my amazing
life, which will be the first book ever to be
published in invisible ink

b) receiving a high-frequency coded radio
message from an agent in the field

28

c) debriefing a mole in my soundproof study.
(To debrief is to listen to a juicy story.
A mole is a spy slipped into the enemy's camp
to search out, and pass on, its most closely
guarded secrets.)

3. If, on the other hand, six pineapples
are lined up on my front doorstep it means
you may come round at six o'clock to help me
feed the carrier pigeons I keep on my roof,
or just to share a tub of ice cream, preferably chocolate flavored.

4. Please make sure you are not being followed before entering my safe house.

5. In fact, I would rather you approached
my house walking backwards, so that hidden
watchers would think you were leaving, not
entering.

(signed)
X. BARNABY DINGLEBAT
Master Spy

Chapter 7

Back at Privilege House on Monday morning, Jacob Two-Two and the other boys had to contend once more with their new headmaster, the dreaded Mr. I.M. Greedyguts, who prowled the school halls searching for boys with shirt-tails hanging out, faces unwashed or shoes unshined, or with jacket buttons missing. He could often be seen munching on a chocolate bar that he had seized from one of the boys. "Bad for your teeth. Hand it over immediately, child."

Mr. I.M. Greedyguts was rumored to be sweet on Miss Sour Pickle, and vice versa, but that was the least of the boys' problems. That was nothing compared to the daily ordeal of their school lunches that were now provided by Perfectly Loathsome Leo Louse. These lunches were either tasteless, horrible, or just plain disgusting, depending on the day of the week.

No sooner did the boys sit down to lunch that Monday than Mr. I.M. Greedyguts rose from his multi-pillowed throne at the head table, his triple chins wobbling, his huge stomach quaking, and called out, "What do we say before we dig in, my darlings?"

"YUMMY, YUMMY, SAYS MY TUMMY!" the boys chorused back, some of them holding their noses.

"These delicious lunches," proclaimed Mr. I.M. Greedyguts, "rich in vitamins, swimming in minerals, are prepared for your benefit, at great expense, by an expert in the field, Perfectly Loathsome Leo Louse." Then he cupped a hand to his ear and waited.

"Applaud," shrieked Miss Sour Pickle. "Clap hands at once, boys."

The boys applauded.

"And how do we show how grateful we are, children?" demanded Mr. I.M. Greedyguts.

"WE EAT EVERY LAST MORSEL ON OUR PLATES!" they answered in unison.

Miss Lapointe, the French teacher, who sat at Jacob Two-Two's table, whispered, "You had better do what he says, children." But she shed a tear on their behalf.

Watery soup was followed by itsy-bitsy chunks of fatty meat floating in a lukewarm muddy sauce. The bread rolls were either three days old or came from a cement factory and dessert was a mashed brown mush.

"What's this supposed to be?" asked Jacob Two-Two.

"Why, it's banana supreme," said Miss Sour Pickle.

"Ugh," said Jacob Two-Two. "Ugh."

Another boy at the table, Mickey Horowitz, groaned.

Robby Burton crossed his eyes.

"I'm going to be sick," said Chris Lucas.

What made matters worse for the boys was that every day, their eyes filled with longing, they had to watch as a special luncheon tray was wheeled in for Mr. I.M. Greedyguts. Today it was a sizzling two-inch-thick rib steak, served with a mountain of crisp French fries, and followed by a foot-high banana split, topped with hot chocolate sauce.

"Unfortunately," explained Mr. I.M. Greedyguts, "I suffer from ulcers, dyspepsia, stomach acid, heartburn, constipation, gas, iron, aluminum, tin, and zinc deficiencies, and allergies too numerous to mention, and can only look on in envy at your daily gourmet repast."

Then, after he had gobbled up everything on his plate, washing each mouthful down with red wine, he belched loudly three times, stifled a yawn, and then made his usual announcement: "I am not to be disturbed in my office for the next hour, as I have important papers to go through."

But even as the sleepy Mr. I.M. Greedyguts prepared to retire to his office, where the hall outside would soon resound with his snores, a pencil-thin Miss Sour Pickle stood up and said, "Mr. Greedyguts, sir, I have to report that Jacob Two-Two has been unspeakably rude to you."

"What's that?"

"Behind your back, Your Honor," she said. "As you were crossing the schoolyard this morning. He stuck out his tongue at you."

"He did, did he?" An outraged Mr. I.M. Greedyguts glared at Jacob Two-Two. "You are lucky we haven't got dungeons here," he said, "as we had during my army days. Or that, because of meddling, sentimental do-gooders, the Chinese water torture is now illegal. And I am also no longer allowed to make a bad boy stand at attention outside — preferably during a thunderstorm or, better still, a blizzard — for, say, eight hours. So your punishment will require some thought . . ."

As Jacob Two-Two held his breath, Mr. I.M. Greedyguts began to pace up and down.

"Wait! I've got it! Oh, yippee for you, Greedyguts," he said, rubbing his hands together gleefully. "Beginning tomorrow —" He broke off, heaving with laughter. "Starting tomorrow —" And he broke off again, quaking. "Commencing on the next school day, and continuing for the rest of the week, you, Jacob Two-Two, as appropriate to a boy who says most things twice, will be obliged to eat two portions of every delicious luncheon served here, prepared for your pleasure in the incomparable, award-winning kitchens of Perfectly Loathsome Leo Louse."

"Oh, no," said Jacob Two-Two. "Oh, no."

"Oh, yes," said Mr. I.M. Greedyguts.

After school, as the boys waited to be collected by their mothers, Jacob Two-Two, Mickey, Robby, and Chris met in the yard.

"Oh, my stomach still aches," said Robby. "Whatever are we going to do about these lunches?"

"I complained to my mother," said Chris, "and she said children today are spoiled rotten, and that's the problem."

"My father just laughed," said Mickey.

"Well, my father is different," said Jacob Two-Two, "and I'm going to tell him what's been going on here since Mr. Greedyguts became headmaster. And I'll bet he'll do something about it. I'll bet he will."

Chapter 8

Jacob Two-Two considered his father a pal. After
he had finished work, he often took Jacob Two-Two out for a
walk.

The next afternoon, in fact, they wandered as far as his
father's old neighborhood, which Noah had once described as
DADDY'S HARD TIMES TOUR, a trip each child in the family had
to endure at least once, obliged only to say "oooh" or "aaah"
at the right moments. Now Jacob Two-Two told his father that

in the week since the dreaded Mr. I.M. Greedyguts had been appointed headmaster of Privilege House, the lunches they had to eat were either tasteless, horrible, or downright disgusting, and sometimes all three, and he went on to describe a few.

"Aw," said Jacob Two-Two's father, "you only feel that way because your mother cooks such delicious meals for us. It can't be that bad."

"But it is," said Jacob Two-Two. "It is."

"Why when I was your age, the school I attended didn't even serve lunch to the children. No sirree. I had to get up in the wintry dark, shake out the ice that had formed on my blanket during the night, and make my own lunch. Usually a lettuce sandwich made with one-day-old bread, which my mother could buy more cheaply than fresh bread."

"Oooh," said Jacob Two-Two. "Oooh."

"And sometimes," said his father, "I had to share that stale bread sandwich with boys who were even poorer than we were."

"Aaah," said Jacob Two-Two. "Aaah."

"You see that building over there?" said his father, pausing to blow his nose. "It's the Stuart Biscuit Company. When I was your age, they used to let us in a side door, where we could buy a bag of broken biscuits for two cents, and sometimes a couple of us chipped in to buy a bag."

"Oooh," said Jacob Two-Two. "Oooh."

On the next street Jacob Two-Two's father said, "In winter, we used to play street hockey out here, using a piece of coal for a puck, because that's all we could afford."

"Aaah," said Jacob Two-Two. "Aaah."

"And when the game was over, we'd fight over who got to keep the piece of coal, which could be added to the furnace fires that kept our homes from freezing. Now, you, on the other hand, are lucky enough to attend the most expensive private school in town. So I don't want to hear any more complaints about your lunches. As it happens, they are prepared by my old schoolfriend Perfectly Loathsome Leo Louse, who enjoys an excellent reputation as a cook."

When they got home Jacob Two-Two took his problem to his mother.

"Well now," she said, opening the oven to test a baked potato, "you must remember that the starving children of Africa would be grateful for any kind of school lunch. And isn't it possible that you're exaggerating, darling, if only just a little?"

"No, I'm not. I'm not."

"Jake, if I talk to you any more now, our dinner will burn."

So Jacob Two-Two raced to the CHILD POWER Command Tent in the backyard to consult with the dynamic duo, Noah and Emma, alias the fearless O'Toole and the intrepid Shapiro.

"What did you bring us?" asked Emma, blocking the entrance.

"A problem," said Jacob Two-Two, pushing past her. "A problem." And then he told them about it.

"CHILD POWER is overwhelmed with problems these days," said the fearless O'Toole, alias Noah.

"Busy, busy, busy," said the intrepid Shapiro, alias Emma.

"We have a report of a babysitter who raids refrigerators and then blames it on the kids left in her charge."

"Then there's the case of the apartment building that won't rent to families whose kids keep rabbits, gerbils, snakes, cats, hamsters, canaries, dogs, or other pets."

"But I'm your brother," said Jacob Two-Two. "My problem should come first."

"If you don't care for your school lunches why don't *you* do something about it?"

"Me?" Jacob Two-Two asked, startled. "But I'm so little."

"We will only help you once you've learned to help yourself," said the fearless O'Toole.

"You're no longer a baby," said the intrepid Shapiro.

There was only one thing for it now, thought Jacob Two-Two. He would have to take his problem to his new friend, Mr. Dinglebat. But as he approached the house next door, he noticed a huge yellow balloon tied to the trunk of the maple tree on the front lawn. That meant Mr. Dinglebat was away on a secret and undoubtedly dangerous mission, and there was no saying when he would return. *Whatever am I going to do?* thought Jacob Two-Two, trudging home for dinner. *Whatever am I going to do?*

Chapter 9

The next morning at Privilege House, Miss Sour Pickle caught Jacob Two-Two daydreaming during geography class. Sneaking up behind him, she demanded, "Jacob Two-Two, I want you to tell me the names of the capital cities of Fiji, Taiwan, and Liberia before I count to five. Onetwothreefourfive."

"Don't know," said Jacob Two-Two twice.

"In that case, you will stay in for an hour after school today," she said, smiling sweetly.

Hiding behind a locker about an hour later, Mr. I.M. Greedyguts saw Mickey Horowitz reach into his jacket pocket to unwrap a bagel smothered in cream cheese. Mickey was just about to bite into it when the headmaster pounced. "Mustn't spoil your appetite for lunch," he said, snatching it away and popping it into his own mouth.

At lunch, Mr. I.M. Greedyguts rose from his multi-pillowed throne at the head table, burped loudly, wiped his three wobbly chins on his sleeve, and called out, "What do we say before we start pigging it, boys?"

"THREE CHEERS FOR MR. I.M. GREEDYGUTS, FROM WHOM ALL GOOD THINGS FLOW!" they chorused back.

For lunch the boys were served soup made from hot water poured over a carrot, followed by rubbery chicken legs with boiled potatoes that were raw in the middle and, for dessert, gluey rice pudding; and Jacob Two-Two was served two portions of each, which just about made him sick to his stomach.

"Poor Jacob," said Miss Lapointe.

Meanwhile, Mr. I.M. Greedyguts devoured a whole roast turkey with chestnut stuffing, washed down with a bottle of champagne, and followed by an entire cheesecake. Staggering to his feet, yawning, he said, "I am not to be disturbed for the next hour," and then he waddled out of the dining hall.

At three o'clock Mr I.M. Greedyguts came upon Chris Lucas

reaching into his locker for a can of Coca-Cola. "I'll take that," said Mr. I.M. Greedyguts, gulping it down.

When Jacob Two-Two got home that day, his stomach still aching, he was told that a letter had arrived for him. The envelope was empty, just as he expected. But, with Marfa's help, he heated a kettle and steamed the stamp off the envelope. Then he was able to read the secret message underneath. "Back Friday. X. Barnaby Dinglebat, Master Spy."

Chapter 10

When Jacob Two-Two's mother pulled into their driveway on Friday afternoon, after driving him home from school, Jacob was delighted to notice not six, but five pineapples set out on Mr. Dinglebat's front doorstep. "I'm going to visit Mr. Dinglebat now, Mummy," he said.

"Are you sure he won't mind your dropping in just like that?"

"Oh yes, I'm sure."

Poor Mr. Dinglebat was in a state. He had, he told Jacob Two-

Two, recently invested a good deal of money in buying Canadian military secrets, and now he was stuck with them. "No customers," he said.

Mr. Dinglebat showed Jacob Two-Two the ad he had placed in *The Certified Snooper's Monthly Journal*:

ONCE IN A LIFETIME OFFER

BUY ONE CANADIAN MILITARY SECRET

GET ONE FREE!!!

Write to X. Barnaby Dinglebat

Master Spy

But there were no offers. "Not even a nibble," said Mr. Dinglebat. "But, fortunately, my dear boy, I have another source of funds. Wait for me here."

Mr. Dinglebat retreated into his dressing room and, when he emerged again, he was wearing an Afro wig, an earring, mirrored sunglasses, a sheepskin vest, numerous gold chains, purple trousers, and yellow platform shoes. "In this outfit," he said, "nobody will give me a second look downtown, and that's where we're headed. I can now safely join the passing parade, where I will appear to be merely another misunderstood, unappreciated teenager, who is getting no satisfaction, to quote the teenagers' great poet, Mr. Mick Jagger."

They walked as far as the Royal Bank of Canada building on Sherbrooke Street. "Is there anybody following us?" whispered Mr. Dinglebat.

44

"No."

"*Are you sure, Jacob?*"

"Yes."

"Are there no unmarked police patrol cars or low-flying army helicopters in sight?"

"No."

"Come with me, then, dear boy. Quickly!"

They entered the bank's lobby.

"You see this thing there?" said Mr. Dinglebat. "That's my personal, top-secret, state-of-the-art, money-making machine. Watch this."

Mr. Dinglebat turned around three times, clapped his hands twice, stood on his head, kicking his heels, then righted himself and inserted a plastic card into the machine, punched out some numbers, and recited:

"Abracadabra,
kalamazoo,
let's have some cash,
to treat Jacob Two-Two."

Next he told Jacob Two-Two to close his eyes and count to ten backwards, and, when Jacob opened his eyes again, Mr. Dinglebat was holding a handful of money. "Holy mackerel," said Mr. Dinglebat, "*c'est vraiment incroyable!* It's *wunderbar! Magnifico!* We now possess sufficient loot to hire a charabanc to transport us to Schwartz's delicatessen on the roaring Main,

46

and get us some piping-hot, luscious smoked-meat sandwiches on rye, with golden French fries and sour pickles on the side. But first, *amigo*," he said, pointing to the phone, "you must phone your mater to request permission to accompany me on this expedition."

Jacob Two-Two's mother said it was okay, so he and Mr. Dinglebat took a taxi to Schwartz's and walked backwards together through the front door, just in case they were being followed by enemy agents, who would then think they were leaving, rather than entering.

Only after they had eaten their fill did Mr. Dinglebat notice that Jacob Two-Two seemed sad. "You appear *triste, compañero mio*," he said. "Down in the mouth. Out of sorts. What ails you, dear boy?"

"Tonight's the night of my father's weekly poker game."

"Surely you wouldn't deny your esteemed papa an evening's amusement?"

"It's not that," said Jacob Two-Two. "It means Perfectly Loathsome Leo Louse will be coming to our house."

"I take it you are not favorably disposed to this gentleman?"

Jacob Two-Two explained that Perfectly Loathsome Leo was always playing nasty tricks on him and, furthermore, he had recently been hired by Privilege House's new headmaster, the dreaded Mr. I.M. Greedyguts, to provide their school lunches. And those lunches were either tasteless, horrible, or disgusting, depending on the day of the week. "Robby, Chris, Mickey, and I told our parents about it," said Jacob Two-Two, "but they either laughed, or said we were lucky to be at such an expensive school, or said we were exaggerating. But we aren't. Honestly."

"I see."

"If only a man like you, a real master spy, could help us to do something about it, Mr. Dinglebat, why I would mow your lawn every week and run errands for you."

"If we are going to mount an operation to do something about your school meals, it will require some thought. Some advance planning."

"Then you will help us, Mr. Dinglebat!"

"I'll think about it. But, meanwhile, *mon vieux*, I hope you realize that it is not for nothing that your friend is internationally renowned, feared by villains in Europe, Asia, America North and South, and the East Near and Far. Let me tell you how I once escaped the death of a thousand cuts that was to be administered by the Sultan of Morocco's personal guard. There I was, tied hand and foot, watching the swordsmen sharpen their weapons, when the sultan asked, 'Any last words, Dinglebat?' 'Sultan,' I said, 'if I were to put in your hands a trick that would enable you to win sacks of gold, as well as amaze your friends, if you have any, would you spare my life?' 'Yes,' he said. So I taught him how to play the Clairvoyant's Gamble, and here I am to tell the tale."

"What's a clair-voy-ant?" asked Jacob Two-Two twice.

"It's somebody who can see things concealed from the sight of ordinary mortals, and it's by playing the Clairvoyant's

Gamble, Jacob, that you will make Perfectly Loathsome Leo Louse look foolish tonight."

"How?" asked Jacob Two-Two, eager for revenge, no matter what the risk. "How?"

Lowering his voice to a whisper, Mr. Dinglebat explained.

"But what if it doesn't work?" asked Jacob Two-Two.

"It's fail-safe, 100-per-cent guaranteed, my dear boy."

"I could get nervous and mix things up."

"But it is also a gamble."

"I'm scared."

"Good. Because no secret agent worthy of his name ever went into action without being frightened. Now we will practice the procedures together all the way home. Okay?"

"Okay. Okay."

"And then, Jacob, do as I instruct you, and we shall prevail tonight. Promise?"

"Promise," said Jacob Two-Two, gulping twice. He was worried, very worried, because he was still a little boy who never got anything right. Ask Noah. Ask Emma.

Ask anybody.

Chapter 11

All the poker players had arrived by the time Jacob Two-Two got home, but they hadn't started their game yet. "Hiya there, Jacob," sang out Perfectly Loathsome Leo Louse. "I was just telling the gang that you enjoy my school meals so much you insist on double portions every day." And then he laughed heartily at his own joke.

Jacob Two-Two retreated to the kitchen, where he was soon joined by Perfectly Loathsome Leo Louse, delighted to catch him alone. "I brought you a present," said Perfectly Loathsome Leo. "Put out your hand and close your eyes."

An apprehensive Jacob Two-Two did as he was asked, and then Perfectly Loathsome Leo Louse popped a wet slippery peach pit out of his mouth and dumped it into Jacob Two-Two's hand. "Tricked you again, didn't I? Now be a good kid and drop that in the garbage."

Jacob Two-Two got rid of the disgusting peach pit, washed his hands, and then entered the living room. His heart thumping, he said, "Now I'd like to show *you* a trick, Mr. Louse."

"Ho ho ho. That's rich," said Perfectly Loathsome Leo Louse, winking at the other card players. "What kind of trick, kid?"

"A card trick," said Jacob Two-Two. "A card trick."

"Wowee!"

As everybody, including Daniel, Noah, Emma, and Marfa, watched, Jacob Two-Two lifted the deck of cards off the poker table.

"I want you to pick a card," said Jacob Two-Two, as the others gathered round, "any card. Show it to me, and then I will phone my friend the Clair-voy-ant, and he will tell you which card you picked." And to himself, Jacob Two-Two added, *please, please, let this work.*

"Oh, yeah? Great," said Perfectly Loathsome Leo Louse. "How much money have you got on you?"

"Don't tell him, Jake," said Noah.

"A dollar eighty-five," said Jacob Two-Two.

"Okay. I'll bet you a dollar you can't do that."

"Don't do it, Jake," said Marfa.

"Leave my kid brother alone," said Emma.

"Do I need the kid's dollar?" asked Perfectly Loathsome Leo Louse. "No." Then, turning to the other poker players, he said, "I'm just trying to make things interesting." Next, Perfectly Loathsome Leo Louse picked a card and showed it to Jacob Two-Two. It was the seven of hearts.

Jacob Two-Two, his heart pounding even harder, went to the phone and dialed the number he had memorized. "Hello," he said, his voice trembling just a little, "can you tell me if Mr. Clair-voy-ant is there, please?"

There was a pause.

"Is that you, sir?"

There was another pause.

"Somebody would like to speak to you," said Jacob Two-Two twice.

"This is going to be good," said Perfectly Loathsome Leo Louse. Wiggling his eyebrows at the others, he scooped up the receiver, all smiles, and barked, "Okay, Mr. Clairvoyant, what's the card I'm holding?" And he held the receiver away from his ear so that the others could listen in.

Eerie, outer-space music could be heard over the phone.

"This is the Clairvoyant," said a man in a low, menacing voice. *"Only the Clairvoyant knows where the dinosaurs have gone; why the earth continues to go round the sun, which must be boring, considering how many trips it has already made; and how many glasses of water there are in the*

52

Atlantic Ocean. The Clairvoyant can interpret the past and predict the future. I also sell Canadian military secrets at bargain prices. Your card, amigo, *is the seven of hearts.*"

"Atta boy, Jake," said one of the poker players, slapping him on the back.

"Way to go, kid," said another player.

As everybody roared with laughter, Perfectly Loathsome Leo, his cheeks burning red, slammed down the phone and turned on Jacob Two-Two. "Okay, you were lucky once," he snarled. "But I'll bet you can't do it again."

"Shouldn't you pay up first?" asked Jacob Two-Two's father.

Perfectly Loathsome Leo Louse dug into his pocket for his thick wallet and dropped three dollars on the table. "We're going for double or nothing. If you can do it again, Jacob, four dollars will be yours," he said, "but, if not, all the money is mine."

"You don't have to do that if you don't want to," said Jacob Two-Two's father.

"I want to. I want to."

Perfectly Loathsome Leo Louse picked another card, the jack of clubs, and showed it to Jacob Two-Two. Then he watched closely, as Jacob dialed the number again.

"Sorry," said Jacob Two-Two, "but may I speak with Mr. Clair-voy-ant again?"

There was a pause.

"Hello. Is that you, sir?"

Another pause.

"Somebody wants to talk to you."

Perfectly Loathsome Leo Louse took the receiver and clamped it to his ear.

"Hey, no cheating," said one of the poker players.

"Yeah, hold that phone away from your ear," said another player, "so that we can hear what the Clairvoyant has to say."

"Okay, okay."

The eerie music began to play again, and then the low, menacing voice was heard: *"The Clairvoyant knows if there is life on other planets; why wolves howl at the full moon; and how many miles per hour angels can fly on stormy nights. Beware of the Clairvoyant who can catch comets and throw lightning bolts. Your card, hombre, is the jack of clubs."*

Everybody began to cheer.

"All right, then," said Perfectly Loathsome Leo Louse, slamming down the receiver and forcing himself to smile.

"Hey, Leo, go look in the mirror."

"Yeah, take a look at your face."

"I've never seen a tomato that red."

"The money is yours, Jacob," said Perfectly Loathsome Leo Louse, glaring at him, "for being such a clever little fellow."

Then Perfectly Loathsome Leo Louse sat down to the poker table and quickly lost the first hand. The other players were hard put to control their glee.

"Poor Leo."

"Made to look like a monkey by an eight-year-old."

A rattled Perfectly Loathsome Leo Louse lost money on the next hand as well.

"Hey, Leo, what's the matter with you tonight?" said a player, gathering up all the money in the pot.

"Maybe you ought to consult the Clairvoyant before we play the next hand."

"Very funny. Ho ho ho," said Perfectly Loathsome Leo Louse, and, to himself, he added, *You made me look like a fool, Jacob-Two-Two. And I'll get you for this, oh yes I will.*

That night Jacob Two-Two skipped off to bed happily, unaware that he had made an enemy, and that there was real trouble in store for him. *I did it*, he thought. *I got something right. I got something right even though I'm still little and have to say everything twice, because nobody hears what I say the first time.*

(*If you want to know how Jacob Two-Two did that trick, and how you, too, can amaze your friends by playing the Clairvoyant's Gamble, turn to page 137, but not yet, please.*)

Chapter 12

"I'm going to fix that brat, that lousy little cheater, that eight-year-old swindler!" bellowed Perfectly Loathsome Leo Louse when he got home after the poker game. "If it's the last thing I do!"

He was speaking to his eighty-five-year-old mother, with whom he lived in the basement of an apartment building they owned in the old neighborhood. The sign outside read:

ABSOLUTELY NO CHILDREN ALLOWED HERE.

NO PETS, EITHER.

RENTS PAID IN ADVANCE.

CASH ONLY.

Old Mrs. Louse was seated in her rocking chair in the furnace room, the only well-heated room in the entire building. "How much money did you win tonight, my sweetie-poo?" she demanded eagerly.

"I lost ninety-seven of our hard-earned dollars," said Perfectly Loathsome Leo, tears rolling down his cheeks, and he explained how Jacob Two-Two, that boy criminal, that unspeakable stinker, had so upset him with his trickery, that he had been unable to concentrate on his cards.

"Why, that's terrible," said Mrs. Louse, even as her fifty-two-year-old son climbed onto her lap, sniffling and sucking his thumb. "My poor uggams," she said, stroking his shiny bald head.

It was just about impossible to move within the crowded furnace room. There was a mound of their tenants' green garbage bags, which they hadn't had time to go through yet, searching for treasures. All the magazines they found, for instance, were stacked in a special pile until they were at least a month old, by which time they became acceptable to doctors and dentists, who bought them for a few pennies each to be placed in their waiting rooms. There were also ceiling-

58

high stacks of old newspapers waiting to be sold, and empty Coca-Cola, Pepsi, and beer bottles lined up here, there, and everywhere.

Once a year, Perfectly Loathsome Leo Louse and his mother went on their annual Spring Harvest Holiday. After the snows had melted, they rode through the neighboring mountain country to search the roadside ditches for empty deposit bottles that skiers had flung from their speeding cars the previous winter. They would ride in Perfectly Loathsome Leo's truck, remembering to switch off the ignition and coast down all the hills, saving gas. It was the panel truck with the sign printed on both sides:

PERFECTLY ADORABLE LEO LOUSE'S SCHOOL MEALS
GUARANTEED YUMMY BEYOND COMPARE

The secret of Perfectly Loathsome Leo Louse's popularity with private schools was his discovery, early on, of their golden rule: the more expensive the school fees, the worse the food they served to the children.

On Monday morning, Perfectly Loathsome Leo was still brooding about his losses at the poker table, which he blamed on Jacob Two-Two. That child swindler, that under-age cheat. But he found some comfort flitting about his enormous kitchen, preparing the day's school lunches, with the help of his mother. Testing a spoonful of soup, spitting it out, he said, "This won't do, Mumsy. It's almost tolerable. Let's fill a pail with stagnant dishwater, pour it in, and bring the broth to the boil again."

"Oh, what a wonderful idea, my sweetums," she said.

Dipping a finger into a tub of mashed potatoes, he growled, "Why, this tastes almost decent. Our reputation could be ruined!"

"Think of something," she said.

"I've got it," said Perfectly Loathsome Leo, and he fetched an emergency bucket of gray, almost raw potato lumps that he kept in the refrigerator, and emptied it into the tub. "Stir it well, Mumsy."

"Hee hee hee," she said, "you are a genius, my truly loathsome one."

Ever watchful, Perfectly Loathsome Leo moved on to a stack of sausages. "Just as I feared," he said, "these aren't sufficiently greasy. Let's drown these sausages in hot bacon fat, and cool the pile before delivery."

"You know something, Perfectly Loathsome," his mother cooed, "sometimes I wonder if I really deserve to have been blessed with such an enchanting son."

Perfectly Loathsome Leo was delighted with his mother's five-foot-long meat loaf. "One hundred and ten per cent terrific, Mumsy. You can actually taste the sawdust in it. Where's it going?"

It was going to Privilege House, Jacob Two-Two's school.

"Good-o!" exclaimed Perfectly Loathsome Leo. "Wonderful!" And he danced his mother round the kitchen.

But Perfectly Loathsome Leo's joy was short-lived. That evening as he and his mother sat in the furnace room, counting their rent money for the umpteenth time, he again recalled his hard-earned ninety-seven-dollar loss at the card table, all because of Jacob Two-Two, and he began to moan and groan.

"Whatever can be the matter, precious one?" asked his mother.

"That Jacob Two-Two humiliated me. He made me look like a monkey in front of my friends. I lost all that money only because of him. How am I going to get my revenge?"

"You'll think of something, my heart's delight. Something mean mean mean. Mummykins is counting on you," she cooed.

It was beginning to grow dark.

"But now we had better go tucky-byes, my snookums. Or else," she said, her eyes filled with horror at the thought, "it will be time to switch on the lights. *Burning electricity!* WASTING MONEY!"

Chapter 13

Surprise, surprise. After school that same Monday Jacob Two-Two had actually been invited into the CHILD POWER Command Tent.

"Good to see you," said the intrepid Shapiro.

"Care for a swig of wine?" asked the fearless O'Toole, reaching for the bottle on the table.

"It's only cranberry juice," said Jacob Two-Two.

"Tell us how you worked the Clairvoyant's Gamble," said the intrepid Shapiro.

"And CHILD POWER will help you at Privilege House."

"I can't," said Jacob Two-Two. "I can't."

"Why not?"

"It's a secret."

"In that case, you are on your own," said the fearless O'Toole, and he was invited to leave the tent.

It turned out to be a bad week all around. The school lunches, which were either tasteless, horrible, or disgusting, depending on the day of the week, were now absolutely vile, but at least he didn't have to eat double portions any longer. One day it was fish pie, made more of skin and bones than anything else and paved with a crust you needed an axe to break. Another day it was spaghetti, all the strands stuck together, with a sauce that was obviously boiled ketchup. Miss Lapointe whispered to the boys at her table, "I have written a letter to the editor of the *Daily Doze* to complain about conditions here."

"Will he do anything?" asked Mickey Horowitz.

"We can only hope," said Miss Lapointe.

Meanwhile, the dreaded Mr. I.M. Greedyguts feasted on roast leg of lamb, or a side of poached salmon, or a mound of veal chops, passing on the bones to Miss Sour Pickle.

"Oh, you're too kind, Your Excellency," she would say, blushing.

Every afternoon after school an increasingly sad Jacob Two-Two stopped at his secret mail-drop on Mr. Dinglebat's front lawn, made sure there were no watchers in sight, and then dug into the narrow slot in the maple tree, hoping for a message. Nothing was there. Finally, on Friday, he found a note:

XBD TO JTT:

FOR YOUR EYES ONLY

READ AND DESTROY

Friday afternoon. 1700 hours. Ottawa rules.

Jacob Two-Two immediately tore the note into tiny bits, dropping the pieces into two separate wastebins, as he had been instructed. But he was confused. Ottawa rules, Moscow rules, Washington rules, all jumbled up in his head. Then he remembered that Ottawa rules meant the park. So, at the appointed time, he slipped out of the house and headed for the Ottawa-rules bench in the nearby park. An old tramp was already lying on the bench, snoring, the sports section of the *Daily Doze* spread over his face. "Wake up, Mr. Dinglebat," said Jacob Two-Two, tugging at the big toe that stuck out of a torn running shoe. "Wake up, it's me."

"Darn it," said Mr. Dinglebat, "I was sure I could fool you with this get-up."

"Where have you been all week?" asked Jacob Two-Two twice.

"Since you last saw me, dear boy, I have met with a lady

65

called Martha on Prince Edward Island, and conferred with Prince Edward on Martha's Vineyard. A master spy's work is never done."

"Gosh," said Jacob Two-Two.

"Now I have hit upon a plan that will be the undoing of both the unspeakable Mr. Louse and the dreaded Mr. Greedyguts. You had better read this," said Mr. Dinglebat, handing him a sheet of paper.

It was a note to Miss Lapointe, written by Mr. Dinglebat but signed with the name of Dr. Magnum Frankenstein, a dentist, excusing Jacob Two-Two from classes on Monday afternoon.

"I hope you're not expecting me to hand this in at school," said Jacob Two-Two, alarmed.

"Yours not to reason why," said Mr. Dinglebat.

"But if my mother ever found out, I could get into bad trouble," said Jacob Two-Two. "I could get into bad trouble."

"Trouble is our business, *amigo*. Monday afternoon we're going on what is known in our trade as a fishing expedition. But, don't worry, I'll have you outside Privilege House in time for your mother to pick you up."

"Where to?" asked Jacob Two-Two. "Where to?"

"Time will tell."

"And what's your plan of action?" asked Jacob Two-Two.

Mr. Dinglebat frowned. "Remember what I told you about 'need to know'?"

"In advance of a dangerous mission," recited Jacob Two-Two, "a spy is told only what he needs to know, nothing more, so

66

that if he is captured by the enemy, and tortured, he cannot reveal vital information."

"See you anon," said Mr. Dinglebat, leaping up from the bench and starting home, walking backwards.

After dinner, Jacob Two-Two, a very worried little boy, went out to mow the front lawns. First Mr. Dinglebat's, true to his promise, and then his own. As the poker players began to arrive, they all greeted him warmly, except, of course, Perfectly Loathsome Leo Louse.

"Keep out of my way tonight, you little cheater," he said. "You're bad luck."

Perfectly Loathsome Leo was greeted with guffaws at the card table.

"Don't you want to place another bet with Jacob before we start?" Jacob Two-Two's father asked him.

"Just deal the cards," said Perfectly Loathsome Leo Louse, his face burning red.

"I dunno," said one of the players. "If I were you I'd phone the Clairvoyant before placing any bets."

Everybody laughed.

"Well, I can handle my own cards," said Perfectly Loathsome Leo, and then he saw Jacob Two-Two enter the room. *Brat*, he muttered to himself.

"Hey, Jake," one of the players called out, "pull up a chair. Leo looks like he's going to need help."

"Oh, yeah?" said Leo. "The truth is I'm going to take you all to the cleaners tonight."

But once again Leo, rattled by all the teasing, ended up a loser, dropping seventy-nine hard-earned dollars at the table, and that made him so angry he stormed out of the house without remembering to take home the food left over on the sideboard. *Drat that boy*, he thought, kicking the first lamppost he came to. *Drat him. Drat him. Drat him.*

Chapter 14

Excused from classes on Monday afternoon, Jacob Two-Two hurried over to Mr. Dinglebat's house, as instructed, and found him on the roof, feeding his carrier pigeons.

"At this stage in the operation," said Mr. Dinglebat, "it is advisable to get to know your enemy, taking the measure of the man, catching him unawares, as it were."

"Yes, sir," said Jacob Two-Two.

"Agent-in-training Two-Two, we are going to pay the dreaded Mr. I.M. Greedyguts a visit in his lair."

"Oh, no," said Jacob Two-Two. "Oh, no."

"Don't worry. He'll never recognize you."

Mr. Dinglebat outfitted Jacob Two-Two with a fedora, dark glasses, a handlebar mustache, a T-shirt, jeans, and scuffed tennis shoes. Then he rubbed a mixture of beer and cigarette ash into their clothes. "It's the small details," he said, "that have saved many a boy from being hanged by his thumbs, or from submitting to the Norwegian pickled herring torture."

"What's that?" asked Jacob Two-Two.

"Better you don't know."

A half-hour later the dreaded Mr I.M. Greedyguts was confronted by two men, one tall, one very short. Both wore fedoras, T-shirts, jeans, and scuffed tennis shoes. Both reeked of beer and tobacco. The taller of the two had a notebook in hand. The other one, no more than three feet tall, was weighed down with all manner of cameras and camera equipment.

Recognizing them for what they were, Mr. I.M. Greedyguts barred the door to his office. "I never speak to reporters from the *Daily Doze*," he said, "and I must ask you to warn your editor that if he prints any lies about me and Miss Sour Pickle or the so-called slop I serve the boys for lunch here, I will sue for a hundred million dollars in damages. Now out of here at once. I'm a very busy man."

"You don't understand, *hombre*," said Mr. Dinglebat. "We are from *Ginsburg's*, Canada's National Magazine. We're here

70

because we're planning a cover story on the Outstanding School Headmaster of the Year. But if you're too busy to see us, we'll go quietly."

"No, no, no. Please come in. Make yourselves comfortable, gentlemen," said Mr. I.M. Greedyguts, and then he waddled over to sit down behind his desk.

There was a jar of jellybeans on his desk, a plate of assorted cheeses, and two foot-long Toblerone chocolate bars. The desk's surface was also covered with letters, bills, notes, and an opened diary.

"Something about the little fellow strikes me as familiar," said the dreaded Mr. I.M. Greedyguts and, looking directly at Jacob Two-Two, he added, "Do I know you from somewhere?"

Jacob Two-Two gulped twice.

"Let me introduce you to Jacques Deux-Deux," said Mr. Dinglebat, "two-time winner of the World's Best Midget Photographer Award."

"Possibly," said Mr. I.M. Greedyguts, "Mr. Deux-Deux and I met at Buckingham Palace, where I usually take tea with Her Majesty, Queen Elizabeth, when I'm in England."

"I don't think so," said Jacob Two-Two, remembering to say that only once.

Just then there was a knock at the door. It was a tearful Chris Lucas.

"What can I do for you, boy?" asked Mr. I.M. Greedyguts.

Between sobs, expecting the worst, Chris said, "Miss Sour Pickle asked me to report to you, sir. She says I was the one who wrote MISS SOUR PICKLE IS A SQUEALER on the blackboard."

Mr. I.M. Greedyguts roared with forced laughter, his huge stomach heaving, his triple chins wobbling. "Think nothing of it, my boy, a good tease never hurt anybody."

"I beg your pardon, sir?" said Chris, his eyes widening.

"Catch," sang out Mr. I.M. Greedyguts, tossing him a large chunk of Toblerone chocolate. "And don't forget to come round for a game of ping-pong after classes." Then he thrust the astonished Chris out of his office, whispering, "I'll settle with you later, you nasty little squirt." Then he turned to Jacob Two-Two and Mr. Dinglebat, his smile sickeningly sweet. "I adore the kids here and they love me back like crazy. You ought to hear them at lunch. 'Yummy, yummy, says my tummy.' 'Three cheers for Mr. I.M. Greedyguts.' Etc. etc. etc."

At this point, just as he had been instructed by Mr. Dinglebat, Jacob Two-Two slipped behind Mr. I.M. Greedyguts, pretending to take more pictures of him, but actually focusing his camera on the desk's surface.

"Would you mind if we interviewed some of the boys?" asked Mr. Dinglebat.

"Oh, no," protested Mr. I.M. Greedyguts, mopping sweat from his brow. "You can't do that."

"Why not?" demanded Jacob Two-Two. "Why not?"

"Because, Mr. Deux-Deux, I so cherish their love and respect I intend to keep it a private matter between us, and you guys can quote me on that."

"Is it true," asked Mr. Dinglebat, notepad in hand, "that you are the nephew of Senator Slimy 'Free-loader' Greedyguts, multi-zillionaire chief benefactor of Privilege House and Chairman of the Board?"

"That's not why I got this job," said Mr. I.M. Greedyguts.

"I never suggested such a thing," said Mr. Dinglebat, "but what were your qualifications, exactly?"

"Love, love, love. I adore kids. I say, Deux-Deux, are you sure we haven't met somewhere before? There's something about you . . ."

Mr. Dinglebat stood up. "You understand this is only a preliminary interview. There are other candidates for the Outstanding School Headmaster of the Year, you see."

"If you selected me," said Mr. I.M. Greedyguts, winking, "I'd be willing to show my appreciation, guys."

"Are you suggesting a bribe?" asked Mr. Dinglebat, crossing his legs and aiming his shoe with the hollow heel, a tape recorder the size of a small bar of soap stuffed inside, directly at Mr. I.M. Greedyguts.

"Certainly not."

"How much money were you thinking of?" asked Jacob Two-Two.

What a quick learner, thought Mr. Dinglebat, pleased with his apprentice spy.

"Ah," said Mr. I.M. Greedyguts, "now you guys will be reasonable, won't you? I'm not a rich man."

"We'll think it over," said Mr. Dinglebat. "Oh, incidentally, you wouldn't happen to know of anyone interested in buying some Canadian military secrets, would you?"

"Buy one," said Jacob Two-Two, "and get one free!"

"I don't understand," said Mr. I.M. Greedyguts.

"Never mind. Forget it," said Mr. Dinglebat. "Bye-bye for now."

Chapter 15

The next night, Tuesday, was very special for Perfectly Loathsome Leo Louse and his mother. It was their OFFICIAL SUPER-DOOPER TREASURE HUNT NIGHT. The two of them, chortling away, stayed up after dark in the furnace room, *burning electricity*, going through the twenty bags of garbage collected from the ten apartments in their building, searching for used tea bags that could be redeemed, coffee grounds that could be recycled, refundable tin cans, and other treasures.

"Oh, lookee here, my sunshine," exclaimed Perfectly Loathsome Leo's mother, "I just found a toothpaste tube with a few more squeezes left in it. And, yippety-do-da, three razor blades that can be sharpened good as new, I'll betcha. And how are you doing, my angel?"

An unhappy Perfectly Loathsome Leo Louse moaned, "All I've got so far are some carrot peelings and onion skins, which will do nicely for tomorrow's soup."

"And how about this, my sweetie?" squealed his triumphant mother, waving a leg-of-lamb bone at him.

Perfectly Loathsome Leo didn't respond.

"And, ring-a-ding, talk of winning the lottery," she said, "here's a mayonnaise jar that hasn't been licked clean. Some people must think money grows on trees."

"Uh-huh," said an obviously glum Perfectly Loathsome Leo, his head hanging low.

"I've been looking forward to tonight for days," said his mother, "and now you're ruining it for me." Then, leaping out of her rocking chair, hoisting her skirts, she danced around her son, chanting, "Leo's a party-pooper! Leo's a party-pooper!"

"I am not!"

"Your heart of gold isn't in it tonight. And I hate to say this, honeychild, but you were not concentrating on your work this morning."

"I was so."

"I spied with my little eye somebody loading a bucket of sizzling, golden-brown French fries onto the truck . . ."

"Oh, no!"

"Somebody whose namesy-wamesy begins with the letter 'L' forgot to have them soaked in ice-water first, to make them nice and soggy."

"It won't happen again. I swear it won't."

"Come sit on Mumsy's lap, honeybunch, and tell me why you're feeling so blue."

Perfectly Loathsome Leo snuggled into her lap. "It's that Jacob Two-Two," he wailed. "Because of him I've lost money at the poker table for two weeks in a row. I've got to figure out a way to fix him."

"Does his family love him?"

"Love that little card cheat? They spoil him rotten."

"Then you've got to trick him into doing something that will make his daddy punish him."

"Yes. But what?"

"You'll think of something, my only port in a storm, my bundle of joy, but now we had better turn down the thermostat on the furnace, to save some money, and hit the hay."

Perfectly Loathsome Leo Louse retreated to his room and was soon fast asleep in spite of the cold. But at one a.m. he wakened with a start and, popping his thumb out of his mouth, shouted, "Eureka! I've got it! Jacob Two-Two's goose is cooked!"

He rolled out of bed, got into his overcoat, and tiptoed to the phone. He dialed the police station's emergency number, put on a little boy's voice, and said twice, "This is Jacob Two-Two speaking. I wish to report an armed robbery in progress . . ."

Chapter 16

Earlier that evening, Miss Sour Pickle, wearing her favorite ballroom gown, had entertained the dreaded Mr. I.M. Greedyguts. She had invited him to a candlelit dinner in her apartment. Setting an enormous rib roast of beef on a platter before him, and a bucket of baked potatoes alongside, she called out, "*Bon appétit*," and waited to be served.

Mr. I.M. Greedyguts sliced off a sliver of beef, not much thicker than a Kleenex tissue, flung it at her, and then lifted the roast off the platter and began to dig in, growling with pleasure. Between bites, even as hot fat dribbled down his chins, he allowed, "You may now call me Isadore or Monty or both, for those are my given names."

Miss Sour Pickle, thrilled by the privilege she had just been granted, replied, "And my name is Natasha."

Working his way through the rib roast in no time, gnawing every last morsel on the bones, Mr. I.M. Greedyguts wiped his greasy mouth on Miss Sour Pickle's best white linen tablecloth, blew his nose into his linen napkin, and barked, "That was delish. Absolutely fab. Now be a good girl and bring on the main course, will you, Nat?"

"But I'm afraid that *was* the main course, Monty."

"No kidding," said Mr. I.M. Greedyguts, frowning.

"Would you care for some cheese? Or some chocolate mints, perhaps?"

"Both. Right now."

Mr. I.M. Greedyguts left just after midnight, enabling him to get to his favorite late-night delicatessen before it closed, so that he could relieve his hunger pangs. Miss Sour Pickle, now that she was alone, could indulge in her secret passion: ice hockey.

She had taped that evening's game, Montreal Canadiens vs. the Boston Bruins, but before slipping the tape into her VCR, she hurried into her bedroom and, as was her habit on such occasions, got into her Montreal Canadiens uniform, including a helmet, laced on her skates, fetched her hockey stick out of a closet, fished a six-pack of beer out of the fridge, and then settled into an easy chair in front of her TV set. No sooner did her beloved Canadiens skate out onto the ice than she hollered, "GO, HABS, GO! GO HABS, GO!"

The first period was scrambly, not to her taste, but early in the second period there was some exciting action at last. Patrice Brisebois, a Canadiens defenseman, speared Raymond Bourque of Boston. "ATTA BOY," shouted Miss Sour Pickle, banging her hockey stick against the floor. "TEACH HIM A LESSON, PAT!"

The two players dropped their gloves and began to slug it out. Leaping out of her chair, waving her stick at the TV set, an enthralled Miss Sour Pickle yelled, "SMASH HIM, PAT. PULVERIZE HIM! KNOCK HIS TEETH OUT!"

Which is exactly when three policemen knocked down her door and spilled into her living room, the first one tumbling head over heels, the second tripping and sent sprawling by the third. All three of them were brandishing revolvers.

A terrified Miss Sour Pickle began to scream.

"Don't worry, lady," said the first policeman, retreating a step.

"You're safe now," said the second, the hand that held his revolver shaking.

"J-j-just tell us w-w-where the r-r-r-robbers are," said the third.

"What robbers?" asked Miss Sour Pickle, cowering in a corner.

"I hope they're not too big," said the first policeman.

"Or rough," said the second.

"Or tough," said the third.

"I don't understand," said Miss Sour Pickle.

"I'm Law," said the first policeman.

"I'm Order," said the second.

"And I," said the third, "am the Officer-in-Charge. Go to it, men!"

Law, muttering a prayer to himself, entered the bedroom. "Nobody in there," he said, emerging, and collapsing onto a chair.

Order tiptoed into the kitchen. "Or in here," he said, coming out again.

"In that case," said the Officer-in-Charge, "I think I'll sit down."

"This is an outrage!" protested Miss Sour Pickle. "I demand to know what's going on here!"

"We are responding," said Law.

"— to an emergency call," said Order.

"— that reported an armed robbery in progress in your apartment," said the Officer-in-Charge.

"Well, I certainly made no such call," said Miss Sour Pickle.

Wearily the Officer-in-Charge flipped open his notebook and read aloud: "'This is Jacob Two-Two speaking,' said the caller twice. 'I wish to report an armed robbery in progress at the home of my beloved geography teacher, Miss Sour Pickle. Her address is 3427 Bile Street. You may have to break down her door, but never mind. So long as you hurry. Hurry, please!'"

"He said that, did he?" asked Miss Sour Pickle.

"Yes," said Law.

"He did," said Order.

"Why, that Jacob Two-Two," said Miss Sour Pickle, "just wait until I get my hands on him."

"Hey, that's some outfit you've got on," said the Officer-in-Charge.

"And it isn't," said Law.

"— even," said Order.

"— Hallowe'en," said the Officer-in-Charge.

"The fact is," said Miss Sour Pickle, "I have just returned from a costume party. And you have been misled. There are no robbers here. Now I will thank you to replace my door as best you can before you leave. Good night, gentlemen."

"Good," said Law.

"— night," said Order.

"— Ma'am," said the Officer-in-Charge.

Chapter 17

The next morning a joyful, giggly Perfectly Loathsome Leo Louse phoned Jacob Two-Two's father. "Greetings," he said, "just calling to make sure we're playing poker as usual Friday night."

"Sorry," said Jacob Two-Two's father. "I can't talk now. Have to run."

"Nothing wrong, I hope," said Perfectly Loathsome Leo, hard put to contain his glee.

"I'm not sure. But Mr. I.M. Greedyguts wants us to report to his office with Jacob Two-Two at nine sharp this morning."

"Oh dear," said Perfectly Loathsome Leo Louse, "I hope Jacob hasn't done something very, very bad."

"So do I," said Jacob Two-Two's father.

"Whatever," said Perfectly Loathsome Leo, "you mustn't be too hard on little Jacob. He's such a lovely boy," and then he hung up. *Certainly that stinker Jacob Two-Two will be punished,* he thought. *The police will be on the case now. Maybe he will even have to appear in juvenile court. Oh boy! Oh boy!* he thought, and he was so excited he had to go and pee immediately.

Chapter 18

Gobble, gobble, gobble. An enraged Mr. I.M. Greedyguts, breathing fire, zipped through breakfast in his office at a record pace: a stack of lamb chops, six scrambled eggs, hash browns, and croissants were washed down with a family-sized bottle of Coca-Cola, and were followed by two chocolate éclairs topped with three scoops of strawberry ice cream. "I'm so upset this morning," he said, glaring at Jacob Two-Two's parents, "that I've lost my appetite."

"I can see that," said Jacob Two-Two's father.

"You don't understand," said Mr. I.M. Greedyguts. "I woke up with my stomach rumbling, because I had to go without a decent dinner last night."

"Why, Monty," said an aggrieved Miss Sour Pickle, "how could you?"

"Sorry. Forgot. Don't know what I was saying. But now I'm bound to suffer from indigestion for the rest of the day."

"No wonder," said Jacob Two-Two's mother.

Mr. I.M. Greedyguts belched twice, farted once, and then pointed a finger thick as a sausage at Jacob Two-Two. "All because this hoodlum," he said, "this criminal born and bred, sneaked out of his bed after midnight last night, phoned the police, and was responsible for a SWAT team hitting Miss Sour Pickle's apartment."

Miss Sour Pickle wiped tears from her eyes. "There I was in my nightie," she said, "when they broke down my door."

"This poor, dedicated woman," said the dreaded Mr. I.M. Greedyguts. "This dear soul could have died of a heart attack, and that stinker, your son, would have been guilty of cold-blooded, premeditated, first-, second-, third-, or fourth-degree murder. How about that?"

"I didn't do it," said Jacob Two-Two. "I didn't do it."

"Liar, liar, liar!" shouted Mr. I.M. Greedyguts, banging his fist against his desk.

"Now hold on a minute," said Jacob Two-Two's father.

"If Jacob Two-Two says he didn't do it," said his mother, "he didn't do it."

"You would say that, being his mother," said Mr. I.M. Greedyguts.

"Our children were brought up to tell the truth, no matter what," said Jacob Two-Two's mother.

"Fiddlesticks," said Miss Sour Pickle. "Stuff and nonsense. I expect you to pay for my new door, and the treatment prescribed by my doctor to deal with my state of shock."

"And what did your doctor prescribe?" asked Jacob Two-Two's father.

"A round-the-world cruise," said Miss Sour Pickle, "where I could kick up my heels on long nights, dancing the boog-a-loo, the boogie-woogie, the conga, and the tango, and, of course," she said, smoothing her tartan-plaid skirt, "improve my knowledge of geography."

"But I didn't *do it!*" said Jacob Two-Two. "It was somebody *pretending* to be me."

"Blah blah blah," said Mr. I.M. Greedyguts. "You will stay in after school for the next two months to wash blackboards, clean toilets, sweep the schoolyard, and perform other necessary chores."

"But what if he's innocent?" asked Jacob Two-Two's mother.

"Furthermore," said Mr. I.M. Greedyguts, looking directly at Jacob Two-Two's father, "I expect you to punish him in a proper manner at home. If you don't own a strap, I can lend you mine. Wham, wham, wham!"

"Look here," said Jacob Two-Two's father, "We don't need your advice about how to bring up our children." Then, turning to Jacob, he said, "Jake, would you leave the room, please. I would like to have a word with your esteemed headmaster."

Jacob did as he was asked.

"A round-the-world cruise," sang out Miss Sour Pickle, "where I could dance the cha-cha-cha, the jig, the fox-trot, the can-can, the polka, the lindy-hop, and rock 'n' roll by the light of the silvery moon with the man of my dreams."

Mr. I.M. Greedyguts blushed.

"Look here, Miss Sour Pickle," said Jacob Two-Two's father, "if you are intent on a round-the-world cruise, you had better start saving your pennies, because I wouldn't even consider paying your taxi fare to the ship. As for you, Greedyguts, let me tell you Jacob may be many things, but stupid isn't one of them. Has it ever occurred to you that if he were to make such a phone call he is far too bright to have given the police his name?"

"All the evidence points to your son as the guilty party."

"Okay," said Jacob Two-Two's father, "let's say, for the sake of argument, that Jacob did make that phone call, not that I'm admitting it for a minute . . . but weren't you ever a mischievous little boy?"

"Why, when I was a shining morning face, I never played with anything but educational toys. I didn't read comic books, or even waste time watching hockey games on television."

"Which have become increasingly violent," said Miss Sour Pickle in a disapproving voice, "setting a bad example."

"The report I brought home from school every month had a gold star pasted to it. I was a Queen's Scout. I won the Junior Red Cross Hygiene Badge. I never ate with my elbows on the table, or peed on the toilet seat, *or stuck out my tongue at the school headmaster behind his back.*"

"I caught your son at it," said Miss Sour Pickle to Jacob Two-Two's father.

"And, as an adult, I'm proud to say, I have never indulged in bad language, tobacco, or hard liquor. I don't even jaywalk. I floss my teeth every morning without fail. And now, if you don't mind, I am a very busy headmaster. Case dismissed."

"Before I'm through with you, Greedyguts, you're the one who may be dismissed."

"Oh, yeah. What for?"

"For not being qualified to have children entrusted to your care."

"Ha ha ha. Ho ho ho. You just happen to be looking at a man who will shortly be featured on the cover of *Ginsburg's,* Canada's National Magazine, named Outstanding School Headmaster of the Year. And now, will you please leave my office at once?"

"I will," said Jacob Two-Two's father. "But you'll be hearing from me."

Chapter 19

T hat afternoon, Jacob was picked up from school by a neighbor, as previously arranged by his parents, who were watching Noah in a basketball game at his school. There, waiting in front of Jacob Two-Two's house, reading comic books, were three policemen.

"I'm Law," said one.

"I'm Order," said another.

"And I," said the third, his chest thrust forward, "am the Officer-in-Charge."

"Pleased to meet you," said Jacob Two-Two. "Pleased to meet you."

"And you, you little squirt," said Law.

"— must be the notorious Jacob Two-Two," said Order.

"Confess."

"Admit it."

"Don't you dare deny it," said the Officer-in-Charge.

"But I didn't. I didn't," said Jacob Two-Two.

"You are charged," said Law.

"— with interrupting our beauty rest last night," said Order.

"And making a phone call," said the Officer-in-Charge, "that required us to go out on a wild-goose chase, breaking into Miss Sour Pickle's apartment. That is a criminal offense."

"I didn't make that phone call!" said Jacob Two-Two twice.

"A likely," said Law.

"— story," said Order.

"And in due course," said the Officer-in-Charge, "you may be obliged . . ."

"— to appear in juvenile court," said Law.

"— before Mr. Justice Rough," said Order.

"— who believes that all children," said the Officer-in-Charge.

"— are guilty," said Law.

"— unless proven," said Order.

"— innocent," said the Officer-in-Charge.

"When my father comes home," said a frightened Jacob Two-Two, "I'm going to tell him everything you said."

A sudden change came over Law, Order, and the Officer-in-Charge.

"Why, you pint-sized criminal," said Law, turning pale, "are you . . ."

"— threatening us?" asked Order, retreating a step.

"He sure is," said the Officer-in-charge, "and that's not very nice."

"It's horrid."

"Shame on you."

"Bully."

Emboldened, Jacob Two-Two pointed at the first car to turn the corner. "There comes my bad-tempered, mean, two-fisted father right now," he said.

"It's every man for himself," said the Officer-in-Charge.

And Law, Order, and the Officer-in-Charge raced for their car, stumbling, leading with the elbows, shoving, and pinching, each one trying to get into the driver's seat.

"It's my turn to drive," said Law, kicking Order in the shin.

"No, it's mine," said Order, pulling Law's cap down over his eyes.

"Forget it," said the Officer-in-Charge, bopping both of them over the head with his nightstick. "I will be driving."

And Law, Order, and the Officer-in-Charge stumbled into their car and were about to drive off, when Jacob Two-Two rapped on the window.

"What is it now?" asked the Officer-in-Charge, lowering his window.

"According to every police TV show I've ever seen," said Jacob Two-Two, "if an emergency call is made to the station, a record is made of the phone number the call came from."

"Are you trying to teach us," asked Law.

"— our own business?" said Order.

"Smarty-pants," said the Officer-in-Charge, and then the car roared off, brakes squealing.

But they had only gone a couple of blocks when the Officer-in-Charge said, "Maybe we should look into it."

"Tomorrow," said Law, yawning.

"Or the day after," said Order, beginning to snore in the back seat.

A brooding Jacob Two-Two was still outside, raking autumn leaves, the first to fall, when he looked up and saw a parachute descending onto the next-door lawn. His heart leaped. It was Mr. Dinglebat, wearing a general's uniform. As soon as he had landed safely, Jacob Two-Two helped him gather in his chute. "Boy, am I ever glad to see you, Mr. Dinglebat!"

"And me, you, dear boy, because we have more work to do."

"I'm in such bad trouble," said Jacob Two-Two, and he told his friend about all the things that had happened to him since they had been to Mr. I.M. Greedyguts' office together.

"Not to worry, *amigo*, because we shall shortly proceed with the second step of our operation. But we will require back-up support. Helpers who are trustworthy."

Chapter 20

That night poor Jacob Two-Two, his sleep troubled, dreamed that he was appearing in court before Mr. Justice Rough. His lawyer was Louis Loser, who was quite the scruffiest, skinniest, and most untidy man Jacob Two-Two had ever seen. He had tangled gray hair and weepy blue eyes. His shirt collar was frayed, and his tie soup-stained. His suit was rumpled. His shoes were scuffed, the laces broken.

Louis Loser had defended Jacob Two-Two in front of Mr.

Justice Rough once before, in an earlier dream, unsuccessfully, of course, enabling him to keep his all-time trial-losing streak intact.

Mr. Justice Rough glared at Louis Loser. "How does your client plead, Loser, you nerd, you disgrace to your profession?"

"Innocent," said Loser in a tiny voice, "if you don't mind?"

"Why should I mind? We're here to see justice done," said Mr. Justice Rough, winking at the jury, "so why don't you make things easy for yourself, you deadbeat, and change his plea to guilty. Think it over. Take your time. I'll give you one second."

"Don't blame me," said Louis Loser, "it's not my fault, Your Honor, but the boy insists that he is not guilty."

"Ha! What do you say to that, members of the jury?" asked Mr. Justice Rough.

"He's wasting our time."

"Insulting our intelligence."

"Sentence the little brat right now and let's be done with it."

Mr. Justice Rough peered down at Jacob Two-Two. "I always knew that you were a hardened criminal and that you'd turn up here again. Jacob Two-Two, you are now a two-time loser, represented by an all-time loser."

"Tell it like it is, judge," called out one member of the jury.

"Right on," exclaimed another.

"What have you got to say for yourself, Two-Two?" asked Mr. Justice Rough.

"I'm innocent," said Jacob Two-Two. "I'm innocent."

"Don't make me laugh," said Mr. Justice Rough. "Why, in all

my years on the bench I've never seen a boy or girl who wasn't guilty of something or other."

"But —"

"I'll wager that before I live to see a little person appear before me who is innocent, I'll find a whale who can play a Beethoven concerto on the piano, or a poodle who can stand on his hind legs and bat .400 in the American League."

"Please, Mr. Loser," said Jacob Two-Two, "say something."

"I don't feel well," said Louis Loser.

"Let me guess what your unspeakable crime is this time," said Mr. Justice Rough. "You were sent down to get something out of the freezer and left the door open *all through the night.* Or you turned up at school with your shirt-tail hanging out. Or you're so dumb you couldn't even tell your geography teacher the name of the capital city of Fiji. Or you were caught reading in bed with a flashlight. I've seen all kinds here. Nothing surprises me any more. Why, earlier today I had a little girl in here, no more than three years old, who wakened her mummy and daddy at three a.m. to ask for a glass of water."

"Shocking," said a member of the jury.

"Incredible," said another.

"Look at my hair, you brat," said Mr. Justice Rough, "and tell me what color it is."

"Gray," said Jacob Two-Two.

"And no wonder! Today I had to deal with a boy, caught red-handed in an elevator in the Ritz Hotel, *pressing every single button, right up to the twenty-eighth floor.* I was confronted with a girl who had sneaked into her mother's bathroom to try out her most expensive perfume and spilt all of it on the floor, stinking up the house. I had a boy who phoned a friend, then forgot to replace the receiver, accidently on purpose, if you ask me, while his poor father was pacing up and down for three hours, waiting for a very important business call."

"Your Honor," began Louis Loser, "I —"

"Hey, Loser," yelled one of the jurors, "tie your shoelaces before you trip over them."

"Did you get that suit at a fire sale?" asked another.

"Now, now," said Mr. Justice Rough, "careful, guys, or this drip of a lawyer will accuse us of being prejudiced against the public enemy he is misrepresenting to the worst of his inability. Order in the court! Order, please! And now let me call upon the prosecutor, an excellent fellow, to state the case against Jacob Two-Two, which I'm sure will be unanswerable."

"Why, thank you, Uncle Justice Rough," said Slugger Meeny, the prosecutor. "Let me begin by saying what an honor it is to appear before you . . ."

Mr. Justice Rough stood up and bowed, acknowledging the jury's applause.

". . . and for openers, just to set the mood," said Slugger Meeny, "I'd like to introduce some witnesses to Jacob Two-Two's very, very bad character."

Miss Sour Pickle, summoned to the witness stand, said, "I caught this brat sticking out his tongue at our beloved headmaster, Mr. I.M. Greedyguts."

"How's that for impertinence, members of the jury?" demanded Mr. Justice Rough.

Members of the jury gasped.

Then the beloved headmaster himself waddled up to the stand, munching on the Biggest Mac anybody had ever seen. "Just the sight of Jacob Two-Two," he said, "is enough to spoil a man's appetite, and I can think of nothing worse to say about him." And then he took a big bite out of his hamburger.

Law, Order, and the Officer-in-Charge were heard from next.

"He resisted," said Law.

"— arrest," said Order.

"— and threatened us," said the Officer-in-Charge, "with violence."

"I think I've heard quite enough," said Mr. Justice Rough. "What do you say, jury?"

"GUILTY! GUILTY! GUILTY!"

Then, just as Mr. Justice Rough was about to sentence him, Jacob Two-Two wakened, calling out, "I'm not guilty! I'm not!" and found that he was safe in his own bedroom. *But where, oh where*, he thought, before sliding into sleep again, *was* CHILD POWER *when I needed them most?*

Chapter 21

At Privilege House the next morning, Jacob Two-Two was caught daydreaming again during geography class. Sneaking up behind him, Miss Sour Pickle roared, "You are not paying attention!"

"Yes, I am," said Jacob Two-Two. "Yes, I am."

"Good. Then you will surely be able to answer the following three easy questions. What is the population of Albania,

103

the principal export of Peru, and how many left-handed people are there in Canada?"

"I don't know."

"Then you will write the following line for me two hundred times — I AM A DAYDREAMER, IGNORANT BEYOND COMPARE — and bring them to me first thing tomorrow morning."

At lunch, the boys, their stomachs growling, watched as a platter of lobsters was wheeled in for Mr. I.M. Greedyguts, followed by a roast goose, a pail of red cabbage, and a potato pie, with a chocolate cake for dessert. "And how do we express our thanks to Perfectly Loathsome Leo Louse for today's feast?" asked Mr. I.M. Greedyguts, cupping a hand to his ear.

"YUMMY, YUMMY, SAYS MY TUMMY!" groaned the boys as they considered their perfectly vile, absolutely yucky lunch: thin potato-peel soup and lukewarm broccoli burgers, followed by a slimy lettuce salad and, for dessert, mouldy bread pudding.

"Oooh," moaned Chris Lucas.

"I can't take this much longer," said Mickey Horowitz.

"Neither can I," said Robby Burton.

"We won't have to take it much longer," said Jacob Two-Two, and he went on to explain that his friend, Mr. Dinglebat, the master spy, was on the case. "He has a plan. He has a plan."

"Good. What is it?" asked Mickey.

"Well, um, I don't know yet."

"Oh," said Chris, obviously disappointed.

In the world of spies, Jacob went on to tell them, everything was on a "need to know" basis, and the need-to-know time hadn't come yet. "But we are going to need your help," said Jacob.

"You can count on us," said Mickey.

After school Jacob Two-Two was presented with a mop and pail and set to washing his classroom floor. Miss Lapointe stopped by to see him. "I want you to know, Jacob, that I and most of the other teachers believe you are innocent. We dislike Mr. I.M. Greedyguts as much as you and the other boys do, but there's nothing we can do about it. His uncle is so powerful."

When Jacob Two-Two finally came home, picked up late by his mother, weary from all his chores, an amazing thing happened. His two older brothers and two older sisters didn't tease him. In fact, suddenly, Marfa, Emma, Noah, and Daniel couldn't do enough for him.

"How would you like to have a lesson on my two-wheel mountain bike?" asked Marfa.

"But I thought I wasn't allowed to touch it," said Jacob Two-Two twice.

Emma offered to set the dining-room table for dinner even though it was Jacob Two-Two who was supposed to be on duty. "You just go and watch some TV, you poor thing."

Noah insisted on writing Jacob Two-Two's lines for him. "Miss Sour Pickle will never know the difference," he said.

"Hey," said Daniel, "why don't we take in a movie together this Saturday afternoon?"

Then Daniel, Noah, Emma, and Marfa appealed to their father at the dinner table. "Do something," they said.

"I have already written a letter of protest," said Jacob Two-Two's father, "to Senator Slimy 'Free-Loader' Greedyguts, who is chairman of the Privilege House board."

"A lot of good that will do," said Jacob Two-Two's mother. "The Senator just happens to be I.M. Greedyguts' uncle."

"Look here, we can't yank Jacob out of Privilege House in mid-term. He'd lose a year before I could get him into another school," said Jacob Two-Two's father. "If my letter doesn't get us anywhere, I will meet with the fathers of Chris, Robby, and Mickey, whose boys are also unhappy, and take things up from there."

Mr. Dinglebat had told Jacob Two-Two that he would require several helpers if his planned operation, whatever it was, had a chance to succeed, so Jacob decided to take a risk. He asked Noah and Emma to meet him in his room after dinner. "I need your help," Jacob Two-Two said. "I want you both to be watchers."

"What's a watcher?" asked Emma.

"It's a spy," explained Jacob Two-Two, "who follows and reports on the enemy, being very, very careful not to be seen." And then he went on to explain that Mr. Dinglebat, the master spy, had come up with an idea for an operation that was risky, but that he hoped would catch both Mr. I.M. Greedyguts and Perfectly Loathsome Leo Louse in the same net.

"What's the idea?" asked Noah.

"Tell us," said Emma.

"*I can't tell you yet*," said Jacob Two-Two impatiently. "Now are you willing to help us or not?"

They hesitated.

"But I can tell you this," said Jacob Two-Two, and then he told how, disguised as the World's Best Midget Photographer, he had accompanied Mr. Dinglebat to Mr. I.M. Greedyguts' office.

"Wow," said Emma, impressed.

"You did that?" said Noah.

"Honestly, I did."

"In that case," said Noah, "the intrepid Shapiro is at your service."

"And so is the fearless O'Toole," said Emma.

"Okay," said Jacob Two-Two, delighted to have CHILD POWER on his side, "then you are to report to Mr. Dinglebat's house at five-thirty sharp tomorrow afternoon."

"Count on me," said Emma.

"And me," said Noah.

"But it is my duty to warn you in advance," said Jacob Two-Two, "that on this mission it's 'Moscow rules.'"

"What's that?" asked Noah.

"If the operation fails, and we are caught," said Jacob Two-Two, "Mr. Dinglebat will deny we were working for him. In fact, he will say he never laid eyes on any of us."

"Gosh," said Emma.

Chapter 22

After his mother drove him home from school the next afternoon, Jacob Two-Two hurried over to Mr. Dinglebat's house and informed him that he had, as requested by Mr. Dinglebat, recruited several reliable watchers, namely the intrepid Shapiro and the fearless O'Toole, as well as Mickey, Chris, and Robby, all of whom would be ready to report for duty when called.

"Bravo," said Mr. Dinglebat. "Well done. And now, while we are waiting, let us look at the evidence we have gathered so far."

First of all, Mr. Dinglebat removed the tape recorder, the size of a small bar of soap, from the hollow heel in his shoe, and played back the interview wherein they had been offered a bribe by the dreaded Mr. I.M. Greedyguts. Then he led Jacob Two-Two into another room, where enormous enlargements of the photographs Jacob had taken of Mr. I.M. Greedyguts' desk hung from a clothesline. "Take a gander at this, *amigo*," said Mr. Dinglebat.

It was an enlargement of a cheque for $1,500 made out to Perfectly Loathsome Leo Louse! "Don't you think that's a bit much for one week's nourishment," asked Mr. Dinglebat, "considering the kind of slop you kids have been eating?"

"I don't understand," said Jacob Two-Two. "I don't understand."

"Let me explain, then. It is my suspicion that once a week Perfectly Loathsome Leo meets with Greedyguts and returns five hundred dollars of that money in cash to your crooked headmaster."

"But why would he do that?"

"It's what's called a bribe, *mon vieux*. It's the price Perfectly Loathsome Leo Louse has to pay for having been awarded the Privilege House food contract in the first place. However, my suspicions are one thing. We require proof. Lots of proof. For starters, we have to catch those two villains in the act. We have to see the money change hands. And then, in good time, we will make them tremble and shake. Meanwhile, feast your eyes on this."

Another enlargement showed that the cheque for $1,500 was clipped to a piece of stationery on which Mr. I.M. Greedyguts had scrawled, MEET YOU AT THE USUAL PLACE, AT THE USUAL TIME, FOR THE USUAL REASONS.

"But where is the usual place?" asked Jacob Two-Two twice.

"I'm glad you asked me that question," said Mr. Dinglebat. "Look at this." The next enlargement revealed Mr. I.M. Greedyguts' open diary with the notation: MCDONALD'S, CORNER OF ATWATER, 6.30 P.M., WEDNESDAY. MEET WITH PLLL. "Which stands for?"

"Perfectly Loathsome Leo Louse," said Jacob Two-Two.

At that very moment the intrepid Shapiro and the fearless O'Toole arrived.

"Hiya, Noah. Hiya, Emma," said Jacob Two-Two.

"Those are not our names today," said Noah.

"Sorry. Forgot," said Jacob, even as they were joined by Chris, Mickey, and Robby, all of whom had already received permission to play at Jacob Two-Two's house after school.

"Gentlemen," said Mr. Dinglebat, "before we proceed with our mission, and let me warn you in advance that it is a dangerous one, you must phone Jacob Two-Two's mother to say I'm treating all of you to dinner at McDonald's tonight."

Jacob Two-Two did as he was asked, adding that they wouldn't be home late.

"Now, Jacob," said Mr. Dinglebat, "explain to your watchers what the procedure is for spies if any of them falls into enemy hands."

"You were never here," said Jacob Two-Two, "and Mr. Dinglebat doesn't know you."

Then Mr. Dinglebat led the watchers into the room where he stored his many disguises, pulled out a long clothing rack, and quickly outfitted all of them with fedoras, dark glasses, trenchcoats, and cellular phones.

"Your assignment, Shapiro and O'Toole, will be Mr. I.M. Greedyguts," said Mr. Dinglebat. "You can pick him up as he leaves Privilege House and, whatever you do, don't lose him." Then he turned to Chris, Mickey, and Robby. "And your man will be Perfectly Loathsome Leo Louse, who can now be found at the Guaranteed Stale Bread Company, on Grub Street, settling his bill for last week's shipment of rock-hard rolls. Stick to him like glue."

The watchers left to take up their posts and then Jacob Two-two and Mr. Dinglebat hurried over to McDonald's and sat down to wait. In order not to call attention to themselves at their command table, they were, of course, disguised. Mr. Dinglebat wore a top hat, a swallow-tailed jacket, a purple velvet cape, and carried his gold-tipped sword cane, just in case. Jacob Two-Two, sporting a safari hat, shoulder-length black dreadlocks, and a Van Dyke beard, wore a heavily studded bomber jacket, black leather trousers, and cowboy boots.

The intrepid Shapiro was the first one to phone in a report

from the field: "Mr. I.M. Greedyguts has just waddled round the corner of Greene Avenue, chewing on a salami."

"Roger," said Jacob Two-Two. "Roger." And then he heard the wail of a police car, coming closer and closer.

"Don't worry," said Mr. Dinglebat. "They are probably headed somewhere else."

But just then the police car pulled up outside, brakes squealing, and out piled Law, Order, and the Officer-in-Charge. Jacob Two-Two froze.

"Act natural, *amigo*," said Mr. Dinglebat, and he dug out the cigarette lighter that could squirt hot pepper, and set it down within easy reach.

Jacob Two-Two gulped twice as Law, Order, and the Officer-in-Charge sauntered right past their table to the counter.

"We'll have," said Law.

"— three Big Macs," said Order.

"— with fries," said the Officer-in-Charge.

Happily, once they had been served, Law, Order, and the Officer-in-Charge got right back into their car and drove off, and Jacob Two-Two began to breathe easier.

Then Mickey, Chris, and Robby were heard from: "Perfectly Loathsome Leo seems to be heading your way. Wait. He has just stopped at the corner." There was a pause. "You're not going to believe this."

"He's not coming," said Jacob Two-Two. "He's not coming."

"*Sh*," said Mr. Dinglebat.

Mickey continued: "There is an old man seated on the

pavement, wearing a sign saying HELP A POOR BLIND MAN, and there is an upsidedown hat held between his knees, filled with coins. Perfectly Loathsome Leo stopped in front of him — looked right — looked left — and then stooped and dug some coins out of the blind man's hat. He is now heading your way fast."

Finally an excited O'Toole reported: "I.M. Greedyguts has just stepped out of Ben and Jerry's, licking a triple-scoop cherry ice cream. The suspect is now approaching the target area. Be careful, Jacob."

Within minutes, Mr. I.M. Greedyguts and Perfectly Loathsome Leo were standing at the counter in McDonald's, placing their orders, unaware that they were being observed, overheard, and recorded by Jacob Two-Two and Mr. Dinglebat.

Mr. I.M. Greedyguts ordered three Big Macs, two buckets of fries, and a large Coke.

"Is that all you're going to have?" asked a disgusted Perfectly Loathsome Leo.

"I'm taking Miss Sour Pickle out for dinner tonight and I don't want to spoil my appetite. What about you, Perfectly Loathsome?"

"Am I paying?"

"Certainly."

"In that case, I'm not hungry."

They sat down at a table, and no sooner did Mr. I.M. Greedyguts finish his snack, than he held out his hand and Perfectly Loathsome Leo passed him a fat envelope.

"The bribe money, no doubt," whispered Mr. Dinglebat, "the five hundred dollars," and click, click, click went Jacob Two-Two's hidden camera.

Then Perfectly Loathsome Leo moved over to the counter where the little plastic packets of ketchup and mustard were available. He scooped up several handfuls and left.

Mr. I.M. Greedyguts started for the door — hesitated — and turned back.

"Yikes," said a terrified Jacob Two-Two. "He's heading our way. *What should I say? What should I say?*"

Mr. I.M. Greedyguts stopped immediately before their table. "I beg your pardon," he said to Jacob Two-Two, "but would you happen to be related to the World's Best Midget Photographer?"

"My friend here doesn't understand English," said Mr. Dinglebat.

"It's just that he looks so familiar," said Mr. I.M. Greedyguts. "Is it possible that I have met the kid at the White House, where I am frequently invited?"

"He's no kid," said Mr. Dinglebat, pretending to be insulted. "My companion here is seventy-two years old."

"Holy smokes," said Mr. I.M. Greedyguts.

"Let me introduce you to Jacoby Zweizwei, the World's Most-Celebrated Shrinking Man. I brought him out of the jungles of Borneo when he was a strapping teenager, six-foot-six in his bare feet. But the poor fellow was bitten by the notorious zitsy-zitsy fly, and he has been shrinking ever since. Why, when

little Zweizwei reaches the age of ninety-two, he will be so *petit*, I will be able to carry him around in my breast pocket."

"Oh, the poor fellow," said Mr. I.M. Greedyguts, leaning over for a closer look at Jacob Two-Two.

"*Don't do that!*" shouted Mr. Dinglebat.

"Why not?" asked Mr. I.M. Greedyguts, jumping back.

"Fortunately, I'm immune. But if he bites *your* finger, you, yourself, will start shrinking. It's contagious, you see."

Mr. I.M. Greedyguts fled, which made Jacob Two-Two laugh. But then he saw that Mr. Dinglebat didn't look pleased.

"I'm afraid we've been outsmarted," said Mr. Dinglebat.

"How come?" asked Jacob Two-Two. "How come?"

"We never really got to see money change hands. I was hoping Greedyguts would take it out of the envelope and count it, but he didn't, darn it!"

"What do we do now?" asked Jacob Two-Two.

"Why, if at first you don't succeed, you try, try, and try again. I will put on my thinking cap and come up with something. Count on it, Jacob."

"I do," said Jacob Two-Two. "I do."

Chapter 23

The following Tuesday, which was OFFICIAL SUPER-DOOPER TREASURE HUNT NIGHT, Perfectly Loathsome Leo Louse and his miserly mum were hard at work as usual in the furnace room, rummaging through their tenants' garbage bags.

"Zowie," called out Perfectly Loathsome Leo, "I just found a used toothbrush."

"And I've got some cabbage leaves that will do very nicely for tomorrow's soup," said his mother.

"Look at this," said Perfectly Loathsome Leo, "some sheets of stationery *that have been written on only on one side*."

"How many, my pumpkin?"

"Seven."

"It warms my heart to see you so happy again, my dumpling, but tell me why you didn't play poker as usual last Friday night?"

"Jacob Two-Two's mother put her foot down. I am no longer welcome there. But do you think I care? No. Why, I hear they're working Jacob Two-Two, that little stinker, so hard after school, that he now has dark circles under his eyes. Har, har, har."

The bell rang.

"You get it," said his mother.

"What if it's the health-department inspector?"

"Wait a minute," she said, leaping out of her rocking chair, "while I empty all the mousetraps."

The bell rang again.

"What about the cockroaches, Mummy?"

"Why, we'll tell them we keep them as house pets. Now answer the door, sweetums," she said, even as she arranged her hair.

Perfectly Loathsome Leo did as he was asked, and he was so nervous he failed to notice the police car parked across the street, three officers keeping watch in the dark.

Perfectly Loathsome Leo and his miserly mum had two visitors. A bent-over old man trailing a long white beard and holding the hand of a fat, freckled little boy with curly red hair, possibly a wig, and red button nose that just might have been false. "Let me introduce myself," wheezed the old man. "You are looking at a world traveler. In my time, I have kept a dog in the town of Moose Jaw, in Canada, and eaten mooseburgers on the Isle of Dogs, in England. In days gone by, I survived on sardines in the city of Kiev, in the Ukraine, and went on to feast on chicken Kiev on the island of Sardinia. To make a long story short, I am a gourmet, an internationally known food expert, and this is my grandson, Jacov Shtyim-Shtyim."

"And we hear," said the freckle-faced little boy, "that you and your mother prepare absolutely delicious meals."

"So we do," said Perfectly Loathsome Leo's miserly mum.

"We are looking for somebody who can cater a dinner for one hundred distinguished guests," said the old man.

"Price is no object," said the boy, just as he had been told to say.

"In that case," said Perfectly Loathsome Leo, beginning to pant with excitement, "you have certainly come to the right place."

"But there's nowhere to sit down," said the old man, heaving a great sigh.

"Leo," said his miserly mum, "take our guests into the parlor and, um, switch on the lights and turn on the heat," she added, handing him the key.

"Do you realize what you are saying, Mumsy?" asked Perfectly Loathsome Leo, because the parlor was seldom used.

"This is a special occasion," she said.

The parlor was a sight to behold. There was a bushel basket filled with little plastic packets of mustard, another overflowing with ketchup packets, and a third spilling over with plastic knives and forks. Sardine tins served as ashtrays. A plastic Javex bottle had been made into a lampstand, with no lampshade covering the light bulb. The ancient sofa was bleeding stuffing, and springs popped through the seat of the only armchair. A rickety table, standing on a tar-paper rug, was strewn with broken cups and saucers, some of them already mended with glue. Over the mantelpiece there hung a photograph of a witch wearing a tall, cone-shaped black hat, a black cape, and riding a broomstick. Underneath, there was a lighted candle.

"Who's that?" asked the boy. "Who's that?"

"Why, this parlor is also our very own museum," said Perfectly Loathsome Leo's miserly mum. "And what you are looking at is a memorial to the Bad Witch of the North, who was unjustly murdered by Dorothy, who struck her down with a flying house in *The Wizard of Oz*, then went on to rob the dead woman of her ruby slippers."

"Gosh," said Jacob Two-Two, tightening his grip on the old man's hand.

"And have you seen this, child?"

It was a riding whip mounted on the wall.

"That is the real whip that was used to beat lazy Black Beauty, when he was employed as a cart horse."

An apple was mounted on a pedestal.

"That is an exact replica of the apple that Snow White, that tiresome child, foolishly took a bite out of. I wish she had eaten all of it, don't you?"

A shotgun was mounted on a wall.

"That's the actual gun that a hunter aimed at Bambi."

"Unfortunately, he missed," said Perfectly Loathsome Leo.

"But we are being such inconsiderate hosts," said his miserly mum. "Can we get you something?"

"A glass of water, perhaps?" suggested Perfectly Loathsome Leo.

"Or possibly the two of you might like to share a peanut," said his miserly mum.

"No, thanks," said Mr. Dinglebat. "But do you think you will be able to cater our dinner party?"

"Certainly!"

"Excellent! *Formidable! Bravissimo!*" said Mr. Dinglebat. "But now I must take my grandson home, and put him to bed. I will leave you this deposit of five hundred dollars as a measure of our good will, and I will be back next week to discuss the menu and costs."

And then Mr. Dinglebat began to count out the money, very slowly, handing an eager Perfectly Loathsome Leo, first of all, a twenty-dollar bill.

Click, click, click went Jacob Two-Two's hidden camera.

"*What was that noise?*" demanded Perfectly Loathsome Leo's miserly mum.

Jacob Two-Two retreated a step.

"The clicking sound?" asked Mr. Dinglebat.

"*Yes.*"

"My false teeth," said Mr. Dinglebat. "Sorry about that." And then he handed Perfectly Loathsome Leo a fifty-dollar bill, holding it up to the bare light bulb.

And Jacob Two-Two's hidden camera went click, click, click again.

"I must see my dentist first thing tomorrow," said Mr. Dinglebat. "But now we must go. *Au revoir. Hasta luego, amigos.*"

Counting their deposit money as soon as their visitors left, Perfectly Loathsome Leo and his miserly mum were too excited to notice *that the bills had been marked with secret signs.* Flinging the money in the air, they danced round and round their parlor, chanting, "Let's raise the rents tomorrow. Let's raise the rents tomorrow."

Then the phone rang.

"Is this," asked the Officer-in-Charge, "number 732-1485?"

"Yes, that's our phone number," said Perfectly Loathsome Leo.

"That's all," said Law.

"— that we want," said Order.

"— to know," said the Officer-in-Charge, hanging up.

Outside, a solemn Mr. Dinglebat turned to Jacob Two-Two. "The trap has been baited, Two-Two, and now all we can do is hope for the best."

"What do you mean?" asked Jacob Two-Two.

"I made secret marks on each of those dollar bills and then photographed them. If that is the five hundred dollars that the Perfectly Loathsome One uses to bribe Mr. I.M. Greedyguts tomorrow evening, we will have the evidence we need. Proof positive that they are both crooks."

"But what you said last time," said Jacob Two-Two, "was that all the proof we needed was to see the money change hands. Any money change hands."

"Quite right," said Mr. Dinglebat, "but this time, my dear boy, it just happens to be my money and I do want it back."

"So that's why you made secret marks on the bills?"

"Yes."

"But what if he doesn't use the money you gave him to pay the bribe?"

"Why, in that case, Jacob, I will be five hundred dollars out of pocket."

"Oh dear," said Jacob Two-Two. "Oh dear."

"Oh dear, indeed."

Chapter 24

The following evening was a Wednesday, when Mr. I.M. Greedyguts and Perfectly Loathsome Leo Louse had their weekly meeting at McDonald's. The Perfectly Loathsome One handed over a thick white envelope.

"If you don't mind, I'm going to count the money right here this time," said Mr. I.M. Greedyguts, narrowing his eyes. "Last week you were short forty dollars."

But as he started to count the money, a flashbulb popped and popped again. Both men froze. Then, Mr. I.M. Greedyguts smiled happily as he saw two men approach their table, both of them wearing fedoras, T-shirts, jeans, scuffed tennis shoes, and reeking of beer and tobacco. "Ah, there you are again at last," said Mr. I.M. Greedyguts. "Perfectly Loathsome, I'd like you to meet a reporter from *Ginsburg's*, Canada's National Magazine, and Mr. Deux-Deux, two-time winner of the World's Best Midget Photographer Award. They're going to name me Outstanding School Headmaster of the Year." Mr. I.M. Greedyguts fished a notepad out of his pocket. "I've been making notes for you, gentlemen, about how I triumphed over a very difficult childhood."

"Why don't we adjourn to your office," said Mr. Dinglebat.

"May I come, too?" asked Perfectly Loathsome Leo.

"Yes, please," said Jacob Two-Two. "Yes, please."

"Just let me finish these last three burgers first," said Mr. I.M. Greedyguts. "Waste not, want not," and he shoveled them into his gaping mouth, one, two, three.

No sooner were they all assembled in Mr. I.M. Greedyguts' office than Mr. Dinglebat proclaimed, pointing at Jacob Two-Two, "*Voilà* Mr. Jacques Deux-Deux, also known as Jacoby Zweizwei and Jacov Shtyim-Shtyim, but actually," he said, ripping off Jacob Two-Two's disguise, "none other than —"

"Jacob Two-Two," exclaimed a horrified Mr. I.M. Greedyguts, his chins wobbling.

"The card cheat," said Perfectly Loathsome Leo, "who was also responsible for the near-fatal heart attack of the good Miss Sour Pickle."

"And I," said Mr. Dinglebat, "am none other than X. Barnaby Dinglebat, renowned master spy, also celebrated as Mr. Clairvoyant." Then, leaning closer to Perfectly Loathsome Leo Louse, he added in a low, menacing voice, "The Clairvoyant can catch comets and throw lightning bolts."

"He can tell you how many miles per hour angels fly on stormy nights," said Jacob Two-Two twice.

"And can offer you," said Mr. Dinglebat, "Canadian military secrets at fire-sale prices."

"Cheaters never prosper," said Perfectly Loathsome Leo, rushing for the office door.

But, lo and behold, his escape was blocked by the intrepid Shapiro and the fearless O'Toole, revealed in Day-Glo blue jeans and flying golden capes, the spine-chilling emblem of CHILD POWER emblazoned on their T-shirts.

"Oh, my God," squealed Perfectly Loathsome Leo, "it's *The Infamous Two*! I've read about them."

"I am O'Toole," announced Noah.

"And I am Shapiro," proclaimed Emma, rippling her muscles.

"They're not — they can't be — the infamous two from CHILD POWER?" squealed Mr. I.M. Greedyguts, digging into his desk drawer for a foot-long Toblerone bar.

Then the office door was flung open and in barged Law, Order, and the Officer-in-Charge, thrusting an irate Miss Sour Pickle before them.

"You, Mr. Louse," said Law.

"— my heart's delight," said Order.

126

"— my sunshine," said the Officer-in-Charge.

"— phoned the police station," said Law, "disturbing our beauty rest."

"And sent us out on a wild-goose chase to Miss Sour Pickle's apartment," said Order.

"And that is a criminal offense," said the Officer-in-Charge.

"Oh, you horrible man," said Miss Sour Pickle. "There I was in my nightie . . ."

"You dare to repeat that charge in public," said Perfectly Loathsome Leo, "and I'll sue you for trillions and ka-zillions."

"Unfortunately for you, my sweetums," said Mr. Dinglebat, "my friends in the police station keep a record of all incoming calls, including the phone numbers."

Perfectly Loathsome Leo began to moan.

"Had you been lucky enough to be trained in spycraft like me," said Jacob Two-Two, "you would have made that call from a pay phone."

"But that would have cost me twenty-five cents," wailed Perfectly Loathsome Leo Louse.

"You saved yourself a quarter," said Law.

"And now you face," said Order.

"— a minimum of ten years in prison," said the Officer-in-Charge.

"Wait," said Miss Sour Pickle, "I will drop all charges if this hoodlum is willing to pay for my round-the-world cruise, enabling me to while away the long hours dancing the twist, the Highland fling, the hora, the *bal masqué*, the square dance, the hula-hula, the Charleston, the bossa nova, and the fandango."

"Would you settle for an all-day canoe trip on the St. Lawrence instead?" asked Perfectly Loathsome Leo. "I'll paddle and provide homemade sandwiches."

"A round-the-world cruise," said Miss Sour Pickle, "first class, on the fabled ship the *QE II*, or you rot in prison for ten years."

"Oooh," moaned Perfectly Loathsome Leo. "Oooh."

"And let me say," said Mr. Dinglebat, "there are other charges you must deal with. Your foul kitchen is infested with mice."

"And cockroaches," said Jacob Two-Two. "And cockroaches."

"Those are household pets," protested Perfectly Loathsome Leo. "My mummy and I respect every living thing. So there."

"We could inform the health department," said Mr. Dinglebat, "and have your school-meals racket closed down just like that. And, of course, you would also have to pay a big fine."

"Maybe as much as five thousand dollars," said Jacob Two-Two.

Perfectly Loathsome Leo Louse's eyes just about popped out of his head. "I'm a poor man," he said, tears streaming down his cheeks, "hardworking, and devoted to my aged mummy. And," he added, "once I've paid for Miss Sour Pickle's cruise, I'll be broke."

"Yippee!" exclaimed Miss Sour Pickle.

"In that case," asked Law.

"— are the charges," asked Order.

"— dropped?" asked the Officer-in-Charge.

"Yes, indeed," said Miss Sour Pickle.

"In that case," said the Officer-in-Charge, "we are no longer needed here."

And, without further ado, the three officers left.

Mr. I.M. Greedyguts cleared his throat. "Mice! Cockroaches! I can't tell you how grateful I am to you, Mr. Dinglebat, and you, too, my dear Jacob Two-Two, not to mention CHILD POWER for revealing what a scoundrel I've been dealing with. Perfectly Loathsome Leo, you're fired! Now I assume that takes care of everything, guys, doesn't it?" he pleaded, reaching for another Toblerone bar.

"Not so fast, Greedyguts," said Mr. Dinglebat, "I think you ought to listen to this. Play the tape, Jacob."

It was the secretly recorded tape of their first interview with Mr. I.M. Greedyguts.

— *If you selected me, I'd be willing to show my appreciation*

— *Are you suggesting a bribe?*

— *Certainly not.*

— *How much money were you thinking of?*

— *Ah, you guys will be reasonable, won't you? I'm not a rich man*

"And that money we photographed you counting in McDonald's," said Mr. Dinglebat, "your weekly five-hundred dollar bribe on the slop Perfectly Loathsome Leo provides you school with, *why, that money was marked.*"

"Hand it over," said Jacob Two-Two, "and we'll show you something."

"The day has not yet dawned," said Mr. I.M. Greedyguts "when I take orders from a little squirt."

"Hand it over," said the intrepid Shapiro.

"Right now," said the fearless O'Toole.

"Yes, sir."

Examining the portrait of Queen Elizabeth on the Canadian twenty-dollar bill, with the help of a magnifying glass lent to him by Mr. Dinglebat, Mr. I.M. Greedyguts noticed, for the first time, that Her Majesty's pearl necklace *was missing three pearls*. Then, peering at a fifty-dollar bill, which featured a portrait of Mackenzie King, he observed that Canada's late, great prime minister was staring at a crystal ball that had been drawn on the banknote. "Holy smokes, I've been framed!" cried Mr. I.M. Greedyguts, his multiple bellies heaving.

"Now, should we phone the *Daily Doze?*" asked Mr. Dinglebat.

"Or bring back the police?" asked Jacob Two-Two.

"Jacob," asked a sobbing Mr. I.M. Greedyguts, "how would you like to skip a grade, and take home a report card every month with as many gold stars as your sweet little heart desires?"

"Hmmn," said Jacob Two-Two. "Hmmn."

"I'm also willing to do your homework for you."

"I think you had better call back the police right now, Mr. Dinglebat," said Jacob Two-Two.

"Couldn't we talk this over?" asked Mr. I.M. Greedyguts.

"Oh, yes, please," said Perfectly Loathsome Leo Louse, falling to his knees.

"Tell them what they have to do, Jacob," said Mr. Dinglebat.

Jacob Two-Two reached into his pocket for the list.

Chapter 25

When the school lunch-bell rang at noon the following Monday, the boys of Privilege House dragged themselves unwillingly, their footsteps heavy, into the dining hall. Imagine their surprise when they found they were being served king-size hot dogs, chili burgers garnished with crisp, golden-brown French fries, and, chocolate ice cream for dessert.

"W-w-would anybody c-c-care for second helpings?" asked a mournful Perfectly Loathsome Leo Louse.

"I do believe," said Jacob Two-Two, "that Mickey would like another chili burger."

"Do you realize how much that costs a pound?" demanded Perfectly Loathsome Leo.

"What did you say?" asked Jacob Two-Two.

"Coming right up," said Perfectly Loathsome Leo.

Mr. I.M. Greedyguts sat in a corner gulping down a teacup full of potato-peel soup. "Finished," he said, holding up his cup. "May I have more, please?"

"No," said Chris.

"Pretty please?"

"No," said Robby.

"But I'm starving!"

Mickey reached for an eyedropper and squeezed eight more drops into Mr. I.M. Greedyguts' cup

"Don't I get anything else?" asked Mr. I.M. Greedyguts.

"Sure," said Robby, fetching him a plate on which there rested one soggy French-fried potato.

"I'm still hungry," whined the no-longer-dreaded Mr. I.M. Greedyguts. "Have a heart, kids."

Miss Lapointe brought him a mushy, brown lettuce salad.

"What about a dessert?" asked Mr. I.M. Greedyguts.

Jacob Two-Two served him two rock-hard, stale raisins and a glass of lukewarm water.

"But what do you say before you dig in?" cried the boys in unison.

"Oh, don't make me do it, please," he begged.

"We want to hear it loud and clear," cried the boys.

"Yummy, yummy, says my tummy," said I.M. Greedyguts.

Then a trembling Perfectly Loathsome Leo Louse asked Jacob Two-Two what the boys wanted for lunch the next day.

"We'll start with ice cream," said Chris.

"Followed by matzo-ball soup," said Mickey.

"And lots more ice cream," said Robby.

"I hope you've written that all down, Perfectly Loathsome Leo," said Jacob Two-Two.

"I'm a ruined man," said Perfectly Loathsome Leo.

Then the boys called out, "THREE CHEERS FOR JACOB TWO-TWO!"

"AND CHILD POWER," yelled Jacob Two-Two. "AND MR. DINGLEBAT, MASTER SPY!"

"HIP-HIP HOORAY!"

An elated Jacob Two-Two got home from school that afternoon just in time to see a helicopter land on Mr. Dinglebat's front lawn, and to catch Mr. Dinglebat emerging from his house, wearing an admiral's uniform and carrying a suitcase.

"Are you off on another mission so soon?" asked Jacob Two-Two.

"Why, before we meet again, *amigo*, I will have sipped sweet water in Sunset Beach, California, and watched the sun set in Sweet Water, Alabama. A master spy's work is never done. Now, you tell your associates in CHILD POWER how much I look forward to working with them again. And, of course, with you, too, Jacob Two-Two, if not today or tomorrow, then before too long, I hope. See you anon, dear boy."

"Come home safely, Mr. Dinglebat," said Jacob Two-Two. "Come home safely, please."

And he stood there, waving, until the helicopter was no more than a dot in the sky.

P.S.

The Clairvoyant's Gamble explained, as promised

Jacob Two-Two phoned Mr. Dinglebat and said, "Hello, can you tell me if Mr. Clair-voy-ant is there, please?"

Then Mr. Dinglebat began to count, "One, two, three, four, five, six, seven —"

When Jacob Two-Two interrupted, "Is that you, Mr. Clair-voy-ant?" Mr. Dinglebat continued, "Clubs, spades, hearts —"

"Somebody would like to speak to you," said Jacob Two-Two.

"Your card, *amigo*," Mr. Dinglebat told Perfectly Loathsome Leo Louse, "is the seven of hearts."

The second time, Jacob Two-Two had said, "Sorry, but may I speak to Mr. Clair-voy-ant again, please?"

Mr. Dinglebat said, "One, two, three, four, five, six, seven, eight, nine, ten, jack —"

"Hello, is that you, Mr. Clair-voy-ant?"

Mr. Dinglebat responded, "Hearts, diamonds, clubs —"

"Somebody wants to talk to you," said Jacob Two-Two.

Perfectly Loathsome Leo grabbed the phone.

"Your card, *hombre*, is the jack of clubs," said Mr. Dinglebat.

MORDECAI RICHLER was born in Montreal in 1931. He moved to England, where he lived until 1972, returning to his native Montreal with his wife and five children. In the Jacob Two-Two books, Jacob and his brothers and sisters have the same names as the author's own children.

Mordecai Richler, one of Canada's most eminent writers, was the author of several highly acclaimed adult novels, short stories, essays, screenplays, and books of non-fiction. He edited anthologies, and was the recipient of several literary awards. He was shortlisted twice for the prestigious Booker Prize, and, in addition to receiving a Commonwealth Writer's Prize, won two Governor-General's Awards for Fiction and the Giller Prize — Canada's highest literary awards.

Mordecai Richler died in 2001 in Montreal.